MY PERFECT HAPPY ENDING

A DREAMY CHRISTMAS ROMANTIC COMEDY...

OLIVIA SPRING

HARTLEY PUBLISHING

AUTHOR'S NOTE/CONTENT WARNING

Please note that one chapter in this book contains a mention of a character's past experience of miscarriage.

1

CASSIE

'**G**ood morning, *chérie*!'

I slowly opened my eyes and saw my husband, Nico, standing beside the bed, flashing his gorgeous smile.

His chiselled bare chest glistened, and as I took in his six-pack, I swallowed hard. I was so lucky to enjoy this view every morning.

'Hey,' I croaked as he leant down to kiss me. 'I haven't brushed my teeth yet!' I winced.

'It does not matter,' he said in his thick French accent before kissing me softly again on the lips. Nico sat down, pulled back the duvet and kissed my stomach. '*Bonjour, mon petit chou.*'

'So today we're calling our baby a little cabbage?' I raised my eyebrow.

'It is cute, *non*?' He ran his hand through his short dark hair. As always, it was glossy and styled to perfection.

'If you say so!' I laughed.

Every day Nico had a different term of endearment. Yesterday he'd called our bump *little chicken*. The day before it was my *little treasure*, which was definitely better than *ma puce*. I'd gasped with horror when I'd realised it meant *my little flea*, but Nico had quickly assured me that it was a common pet name in France. I'd lived in Paris for over a year and a half and was still getting used to the lingo.

'How did you sleep?'

'Apart from feeling like I needed to wee every five minutes, the leg cramps and our *little cabbage* kicking more enthusiastically than a Premier League football player, I slept brilliantly!'

Not.

If I'd had more than a few hours' kip I'd be surprised. It wouldn't be for too much longer, though. In six weeks, our little one would enter the world and we'd finally get to meet our son or daughter.

Nico and I had decided to wait until the birth to find out whether it was a boy or girl. I still couldn't believe I was having a baby.

Two years ago, I was single and unlucky in love. But after literally bumping into Nico in London a few days before Christmas and instantly hating him, that dislike had quickly turned into lust then blossomed into love when I went to Paris a couple of months later.

That summer, Nico proposed, and less than a year later we were married and expecting. It had all happened so quickly, and every day I had to pinch myself to check it was real.

'Sorry that you did not sleep well.' Nico brushed his thumb across my cheek. 'I am happy that our little angel is kicking a lot. It is a good sign, *non*? Not comfortable for you, I am sure, but… would you like me to rub your legs and your feet, to help with the cramps?'

'That would be amazing, thanks!'

Nico sat on the bed beside me. As soon as his hands made contact with my skin, my whole body tingled. I squeezed my eyes shut and a moan escaped my lips.

This feels so good.

Within seconds, I forgot about cramps and lack of sleep as desire flooded my body.

I opened my eyes and bit my lip as I took in the sight of Nico: his broad shoulders, those fitted boxer shorts…

'You know what would also make me feel better?' I reached forward and ran my hands down his abs. Nico froze.

'*Chérie*, it is not a good idea. We have to think about the baby.'

'But it's safe! The doctor said so!'

'Come.' Nico jumped off the bed and headed towards the dressing room. 'Breakfast is ready. You need to eat. It is important to keep you and the baby healthy.'

I blew out a breath. Rejected. Again.

It was crazy. During the first few months, what with all the throwing up, morning sickness (why they call it that when you puke throughout the day is anyone's guess), and generally feeling like shit, the last thing I felt like doing was getting jiggy.

But once the sickness stopped, when it came to sex, I went from 'hell no' to 'hell yeah' with bells on. I was like a dog on heat who wanted to hump Nico every time I saw him. The horny hormones were raging. Trouble was, the bigger I became, the less he wanted to make love.

I thought Nico would love my bigger boobs, but every time I suggested getting it on, Nico shut it down. He'd say it wasn't a good idea, or that he didn't want to hurt the baby. I understood his concern—I mean, Nico was a big boy, but the baby was in a cocoon. It wouldn't feel anything. He wasn't going to pop the amniotic sac with his knob.

It didn't matter how many times I or the doctor told him it would be fine, he still didn't want to.

Maybe it was because of what had happened last time we'd tried. Or he just didn't find my new curves attractive.

Either way, it looked like I'd have to accept that I wasn't going to get any action until after the baby was born, at which point I would probably be too exhausted to want it anyway.

I grabbed my silk dressing gown from the chair beside the bed, slipped my arms into the sleeves, then tied the belt loosely around my big bump.

After buttoning up his crisp white shirt and zipping up his smart navy trousers, Nico scooped me up in his arms.

'What are you doing…?'

'Taking you downstairs to have breakfast.'

'I can walk myself!' Well, hobble might be a more accurate description, but it was fine.

'*Non.* Your legs are hurting. I will carry you.'

I knew that protesting would be pointless, so I buried my head in his chest and inhaled his delicious woody scent instead. If smelling my hubby was the only form of intimacy I'd get today, I was still a lucky lady.

After carrying me down the stairs like I was as light as a feather, Nico strode along the spacious hallway and kicked open the door to the grand dining room. I was still getting used to the fact that I lived somewhere so fancy.

This room was bigger than my entire flat back in London. As usual, there was a spread fit for royalty laid out on the huge stone table.

'*Bonjour*, Cassie.' Fabien, Nico's chef, came in the room holding a glass of freshly squeezed orange juice.

Yeah. Nico had a chef. And a chauffeur. And a bit more money in the bank than the average person…

A *lot* more.

He was a billionaire running Icon, his hairdressing and electrical tools empire, as well as having investments in more successful businesses than I had fingers to count.

'Hi! How are you?'

'I am good. I have made a fresh fruit salad. If there is anything else you need, tell me.'

'*Merci*,' Nico and I said in unison as Fabien nodded, then left.

'So, today I will confirm the chef for the holiday. It is a shame that we cannot bring Fabien, but it is important for my staff to spend time with their families at Christmas.'

'Agreed.'

Our baby was due in January. As this would be our last Christmas as a couple, we had an incredible holiday planned in two weeks' time.

We'd hired a fancy cabin in the Scottish Highlands, which was one of the coolest Christmas destinations. Loads of celebs went there.

It was fully booked for the next three years and the waiting list was longer than the Great Wall of China, so we were lucky to get a reservation. If we didn't go this month, it'd be ages before we'd have the chance to visit.

There'd be twelve of us in total—ten adults and two children. It was going to be epic.

'Tell me'—Nico took a sip of his coffee—'what else do you need for the holiday?'

'I've got it all under control. I've ordered the turkey, all the food and drink, the big Christmas tree and some *gorgeous* decorations. Everything will arrive a few days early, but the manager will store them for us, then move everything into the cabin so that it's ready for when we arrive.'

I used to be a PA, so I loved organising things. Knowing it was always harder to source items at Christmas and that sometimes things were delayed, I'd allowed some contingency time, just in case. Every detail was planned to make sure the whole holiday was perfect.

Funny to think that before I'd met Nico, I hadn't been a fan of Christmas. So many disastrous things had happened to me around the festive season that I was convinced it was cursed. Thankfully that bad luck was in the past.

'Okay.' Nico nodded. 'The chef will also make a menu every day. Perhaps we should check if anyone has allergies?'

'I'm on it. That'll give me something to work on today.'

I'd be glad of the distraction. I'd recently gone on maternity leave from my job working as the head of the Icon Foundation, and I was going a bit stir-crazy sitting at home all day. I wasn't used to not working.

'I saw your email to confirm that the cars and chauffeurs are booked to take everyone from the airport to the cabin. Would you like a masseuse?'

'Wow! Really?'

'Of course. Anything to make sure you are comfortable. And should we organise a Santa Claus and some entertainers for the children?'

'Um… maybe?' I admit, I hadn't thought about that. Nico loved going the extra mile.

'And did you think more about when you will be ready to interview the nanny? We do not have much time to decide before the baby arrives, and then there is the nursery to finish decorating and the—'

'Nico…' I rubbed my temples.

'Is everything okay?' He rested his hand on my back.

'Yes… no, it's just… is it okay if we talk about this later?'

I still hadn't decided what I wanted to do about all that. I needed a few more days to think.

'Understood. I will leave you to eat breakfast. I will work from home this morning, so that I am here if you need me.'

'Darling, it's fine. Go to the office. I'm pregnant, not sick. I'll be okay. Don't worry.' I squeezed his hand.

'If you are sure.' He kissed me on the cheek, then headed to the door. 'Call if you need anything. Odette will arrive soon to take care of you.'

'O-okay… thanks. Enjoy your day.'

Nico meant well, but sometimes I felt like a delicate porcelain doll wrapped in cotton wool.

Ever since we'd first discovered I was pregnant, he'd been extra attentive. Making sure that the baby and I wanted for nothing, which was sweet. But as someone who'd been raised to be independent, I found it hard to be fussed over. It was Nico's way of caring, though.

After growing up in a modest house in South London and spending all my life often struggling to make ends meet, I was still trying to get used to all of the extravagant things that were now available to me.

I mean, Nico just asked if I wanted to hire a masseuse for our holiday. That was so… indulgent. Especially considering we were already having a chef and a load of other treats.

The whole nanny thing was hard to get my head around too. Mum and Dad had worked multiple jobs between them and raised four kids, so it felt a bit OTT to hire a nanny for one child. God knows what they'd say if they knew we were getting one.

After showering I got dressed, then went to relax on the sofa. Odette, the housekeeper, came into the living room. Yeah. We had help around the penthouse too.

'*Bonjour*, Madame Chevalier.'

'Hi, Odette, and please—call me Cassie.' It didn't matter how many times I said she didn't need to be so formal, she always insisted.

'What do you need? More cushions?' She quickly plucked two from the other end of the sofa and rushed to prop them behind my back.

'It's okay,' I said, but she ignored me and did it anyway. I wiped my forehead. Probably shouldn't have worn this cashmere jumper when the heating was on.

'You are hot?' Her face crumpled. She plucked a magazine from the coffee table, then fanned the pages in front of my face.

OMG.

'*Merci*, but I'm okay.'

'But the baby… Monsieur Chevalier said I must do everything to make you comfortable.'

'Odette,' I said softly. '*Merci beaucoup* for your concern, but I'm good. I'm just going to call my mum…'

As Odette stopped fanning me and left the room, my shoulders loosened. I dialled the number.

'So you remember me, do you?' Mum answered in her thick St Lucian accent. 'Now you're a lady of the manor, you don't have time to speak to your own mother.'

'Of course I do! Sorry!'

'When you lived in London, you *always* had time to call me. And your friends.' *Jeez.* I knew I said I'd call her first thing, but it was only ten thirty, which meant it was half nine in London. 'When did you last speak to your cousin?'

'Bella? Last week I think. After I went on maternity leave.'

'You two used to be so close.'

'We are! Why? What have you heard?' My heart thudded in my chest. I hoped she was okay.

'Bella and Mike are having a tough time. Their monthly mortgage payments have shot up and work is slow for her, so they're struggling, financially.'

'I didn't know! Bella didn't say anything.'

'Probably because she thought you wouldn't understand. She probably felt silly complaining about their payments increasing by hundreds of pounds a month when you and Nico earn that in seconds.'

My chest tightened. Bella and I used to tell each other everything and now I was hearing about her situation second-hand? It must be bad if my aunt had spoken to Mum about it.

'I'll call her now. If I'd known, I would've offered to

help.' I always helped my friends and family out financially. We'd paid off my parents' mortgage. When my other bestie Melody was struggling last year, I'd given her money, and I'd do the same for Bella in a heartbeat. She only had to ask.

'Not everyone wants to feel like a charity case. Anyway, I wanted to speak about the hospital arrangements. I'm happy you've decided to give birth in London, but you still haven't told me what hospital you've chosen. Are you thinking of King's College or St Thomas'? I can speak to my old colleagues. Make sure you're looked after.'

Shit. I'd avoided this conversation for ages. It was time to fess up.

'Er… neither. We've kind of arranged for me to give birth in a…' I took a deep breath. 'In a private maternity ward.'

Mum gasped so loudly I thought my eardrums might burst. Thank God I'd left out the part where it was the same place that the royal family used.

And if she knew the cost, she'd pass out. I'd nearly fallen off my chair when I'd seen that the suite Nico had booked was around ten grand a night. They even had a chef and a champagne list to toast the birth of the baby. Crikey.

'A *private* hospital? So you're too good for the NHS now? You and your siblings were born in a normal hospital and you turned out just fine! Sounds like *someone's* getting too big for their boots,' she tutted.

'It's not like that…' I protested.

'I'd better go. We've got friends coming round for lunch, so I need to clean. I imagine it's been a while since *you've* done any housework.' I swallowed hard. She was right. 'I was cooking and cleaning right up to the day I gave birth for all *four* of my pregnancies.'

'If you need help around the house, I can hire someone for you?'

'Not everything is about *money*, Cassie. Remember that. Don't get so swept up in your fancy lifestyle that you take your feet off the ground. And don't forget to call your cousin! Bye.' She hung up.

I sank back on the sofa. I knew she'd be upset. Until she'd retired, Mum had worked as a nurse for the NHS, so me choosing to go private was a betrayal. I was surprised she hadn't called me Judas.

The hospital was Nico's idea. He wasn't doing it to be fancy. Despite being more loaded than a bank vault, he was still really humble. Nico was just so determined to make sure I got the best of everything that sometimes he went a bit overboard, and I didn't want to sound ungrateful.

There was no time to think about that now, though. I needed to check on Bella. I dialled her number. The phone rang out.

Was what Mum said true? Did my friends feel uncomfortable sharing their financial worries because they thought I didn't understand anymore?

She was right about one thing, though. Bella and I didn't message as much as we used to. Same with Melody.

Bella was probably busy teaching, so couldn't answer the phone. I'd text instead.

Me

Hey! How are you? Everything okay?

. . .

I debated whether or not to mention the money thing. I could wait until we spoke on the phone, but if she felt embarrassed about asking for help, that might be more awkward. A text would be better.

Me

Mum mentioned that your mortgage payments have shot up. Sorry to hear that. Happy to help out if you need it? Call when you're free xxx

If I sat inside any longer, I'd start overthinking. I needed a distraction. After grabbing my phone, coat and handbag, I put on my trainers and left.

Maurice, our chauffeur, was waiting downstairs. He jumped out and opened the door.

'*Bonjour*, Cassie, how are you feeling today?'

'Okay, thanks. You?' I climbed inside.

'I am good. Where would you like to go?'

'Just to the café, please.'

'Very well. I will take the scenic route.'

I sat back on the spacious, heated leather seat. The car weaved through the bustling streets. Paris was always busy, but with Christmas fast approaching, it was extra crowded.

As we drove along the Champs-Élysées, there were endless rows of people on each side, and the sound of beeping car horns filled the air. The shop windows were adorned with colourful Christmas decorations and looked so pretty.

It was a shame it was daytime. Despite the crowds and traffic, I loved driving down here during the evenings at this time of year. That was when the City of Light really lived up to its name. The trees lining this iconic avenue sparkled with golden lights and everything looked extra magical. I'd never tire of these views.

My phone pinged.

Bella

Thanks for your message. Yeah, things are a bit tight. Bloody inflation!

I appreciate the offer, but we'll be okay. Hopefully work will pick up after Christmas.

How are you? xxx

I knew Bella would be too proud to ask for help, but I didn't like the thought of her stressing over money when I could give her a hand.

After driving further from the city centre, Maurice pulled up outside my favourite café. I liked coming here. Despite being away from the buzz of the better-known parts of the city, it was always bustling with life.

'You don't have to wait,' I said as Maurice opened the door for me again. He raised his eyebrow and I understood that was out of the question. No doubt Nico had given him strict instructions to babysit me.

The delicious aroma of hot chocolate and coffee flooded my nostrils as soon as I entered the café. It was so warm and inviting.

There were people relaxing at the red-and-white patterned tables and chairs, reading newspapers, staring at their phones or chatting to friends. The ring of happy conversation and laughter vibrated around me.

Once I'd taken a coffee and a pastry out to Maurice, I

picked up my steaming cup of hot chocolate, got comfy in a cosy window seat, then replied to Bella.

Two women pulled out the chairs at the table beside mine. As I heard them speaking English, I smiled. It was always so comforting to hear my mother tongue in Paris.

I tried to work out their accent. *Oooh.* Sounded like they were from South London like me. I was almost tempted to say hello.

'Look at that car!' The lady with bright pink lipstick pointed to the huge shiny black car Maurice had driven me in. 'So fancy.'

'D'you think it belongs to a celeb?' Her friend, who was wearing a bright red Christmas jumper, asked. Nice to see someone was in the festive spirit.

'Maybe!'

'I wonder who it is and where they went?'

I laughed to myself. They'd be so disappointed to know it was just me and not some big A-list star.

'Probably shopping at some fancy boutique or doing brunch, *dar-ling*,' pink lippy lady said in a posh voice.

People watching and conversation eavesdropping was so fun.

'Nah!' Christmas jumper lady shook her head. 'All the fancy shops are down that Champs-Élysées street.'

'Oh yeah! And a rich person wouldn't hang around a normal café.'

'They'd sit in their mansion on their diamond throne and get their minions to get coffee for them.'

'Yeah! They wouldn't have to buy croissants! They'd have a chef to make them, a butler to serve them, then some other lackey to feed them!'

'Ha! Exactly! They'd be like: "Jeeves! Bring me my

coffee! Right now, you little shit! And my organic butter croissants. Now feed them to me on my silver fork two crumbs at a time."' Jumper lady cackled.

'And they'd have someone to sit on their throne ten minutes before they sat on it so it was nice and warm.'

'Or someone to fan them if they're too hot!'

'And a servant to wipe their arse!'

As they erupted into a fit of giggles, I shuffled uncomfortably in my seat, beads of sweat pooling along my hairline.

'Rich people don't know what life is like for us. They don't have to worry about the cost-of-living crisis, increases in mortgage payments or energy prices.'

'I know, right? My weekly shop is ridiculous! I spent a hundred quid the other day and there was barely anything in my trolley!'

'Same! Rich people have more money than they know what to do with. And they spend it on fancy, unnecessary shit when it could be used to help people who really need it. *So* wasteful!'

I swallowed hard. Eavesdropping wasn't so fun after all.

They didn't know I was the person who'd travelled in the car. And they didn't realise how accurate some of their comments were.

I *did* have a chef that made me croissants. And Odette *had* bloody fanned me earlier. She'd never offered to wipe my arse, though, thank God.

And they were right. I didn't have to worry about rising costs as much as my friends did.

Nico and I *did* waste money on fancy crap when that cash could be given to people more deserving. Yes, we already did a load of stuff for charities, especially through our foundation, but should we do more?

I hated to admit it, but what those women had said was what I'd thought about the rich before I'd met Nico. And now I'd become the type of person I used to hate.

Shit.

Was Mum right? Had I gotten too big for my boots?

Take this Christmas trip. Who did I think I was staying in a place that cost more for six nights than I used to earn in a year?

Who spent thousands of pounds on food, drink and decorations for goodness' sake?

And who hired a bloody chef and a team of chauffeurs, masseuses and children's entertainers?

Just because I'd married someone loaded, it didn't mean I should disappear up my own backside by splurging on an elaborate holiday with all the jingle bells and diamond-encrusted whistles.

It was completely over the top, wasteful and unnecessary. That money could give hundreds of people in need a roof over their heads and a hot meal for Christmas. Or pay Bella's mortgage for a year. Probably two.

My stomach churned with disgust.

Like Mum said, not everything was about money. We didn't need to splash the cash to have a good time.

Christmas was supposed to be about togetherness, right? Not material things.

I needed to speak to Nico. Tell him there'd been a change of plan. We didn't need a fancy Christmas holiday with our friends after all…

2

NICO

Although I was supposed to be working, I could not tear my eyes away from the photo on my desk. It was me and Cassie in front of *Le mur des je t'aime*—the I Love You Wall—which was taken when she had first come to visit me in Paris. She looked so happy. I hoped that she was okay.

Maurice had messaged earlier to say that he had taken her to the café. I would prefer that she was at home, where Odette and Fabien could take care of her, but I understood that sometimes she needed a change of scene.

I knew that Cassie found it difficult staying at home and not working. She was not used to this. I also knew that she believed I fussed too much.

And I definitely knew that she was frustrated, sexually.

The look on her face when I had to say no again when she wanted to make love this morning made my heart break. She thought I did not want her. But in fact, the opposite was true.

I wanted my wife more than she knew. More than I

could ever explain to her. I did not believe that it was possible, but she became even more beautiful every day. Seeing her stomach grow, knowing that she was carrying our child—a life that we had created together—was incredibly sexy. But I had to ignore my urges. Especially after what had happened before.

We would have the rest of our lives to enjoy each other's bodies. The most important thing now was making sure that our baby stayed safe. If I did something to hurt our child, I would not forgive myself.

The Christmas holiday would be here soon. This would be good for Cassie. I might not be able to satisfy her in the way that she would like, but being with her friends in a cabin would make her happy. Cassie had wanted to visit this resort since last year, so she was very excited.

The cabin would have everything she needed: the best Christmas tree and decorations. The chef would cook her favourite things (healthy options, of course) and because I knew her legs and back hurt a lot, I would hire the best masseuse to give her massages every day to make her feel better. Nothing would be too much for my wife.

I wanted to give Cassie and our child the world. Everything she deserved and more. I would do whatever was needed to make this holiday perfect.

There was a knock at the door.

'*Oui?*' I answered.

'Hey.' Cassie stepped inside my office. My heart swelled. *Mon Dieu,* she was a vision. Her light brown skin glowed and her thick dark curly hair spilled from her green hat. Since she had become pregnant, it was extra shiny.

As she walked towards me, my chest grew tight. Just half an hour ago, Maurice had told me that Cassie was at the café, but now she had come to the office. This was unusual. I rushed over to her.

'Is something wrong, *chérie*?'

'Yeah.' She stopped. My face fell. I rested my hands on her shoulders.

'Do you not feel well?' I led her over to the sofa. 'Is everything okay with the baby?'

'Yeah, sorry. I didn't mean to worry you—we're both fine. That's not the problem.'

'What is it? Whatever you need, tell me and it will be done.'

'That's the thing…' She paused. I sat beside her. She looked troubled. Like she was trying to find the right words. This was not like my wife at all. She was always direct. It was one of the many things that I loved about her.

'Cassie.' I lifted her chin. 'Tell me.'

'I don't want to sound ungrateful. You do so much already. You've given me so much…'

'You know that I would do anything for you. I would give up everything I own, give my life, anything to keep you safe.'

'I know. And I love you for that. I'm so lucky to have you and share all of these amazing things. We get to travel to incredible places, we have the money to buy lots of beautiful things and I want you to know that I never, ever take that for granted. But, I've been thinking about the holiday. I know it was my idea, but now I'm having second thoughts. It feels… wrong.'

'*Pourquoi?*'

'Because… I know you're minted, but spending all this money seems wasteful. In the current climate it feels too…

extravagant. Out of touch. It's not who I am. It's not who my friends or family are. It's too… flashy.'

'You think I am flashy?'

'No! You're rich, but you're still one of the most down-to-earth people I know and that's another thing that I adore about you. But it's just… my friends are struggling —financially. And we're not used to fancy things. Christmas has always been low-key. Well, not low-key exactly, but just not big and extravagant. I don't want them to think that we're showing off, or being insensitive. I don't want them to think that I've forgotten where I come from and become all la-di-da.'

'I do not understand. Your friends and family came to our wedding, *non*?'

'Course! You know they did!'

'So they did not think that a wedding in a chateau in the South of France with unlimited champagne, five-star dining, a live band, a fireworks display and every expense paid for was not *extravagant*?'

'Well, yeah, but that was different. That was a wedding. Most people push the boat out for that.'

'Push the boat? What does a boat have to do with our wedding?'

'Sorry! It's an English saying: it means to spend a lot of money on stuff.'

'I see.' Since living and working with Cassie, my English had improved, but there were still many British phrases she used that I did not understand.

'Rightly or wrongly, people are kind of used to weddings being fancy. People save up for years for them or take out loans and then probably spend ages paying them off, just for that one special day. Somehow wedding extravagance is socially acceptable, but being flashy at Christmas feels a bit OTT. Especially for someone like me.'

'Someone like you?' I frowned.

'Yeah. Two years ago I hated Christmas. And now we're spending more money than most of my friends earn in a year to celebrate it for five days. We could give that cash to charity or put it to better use.'

I took her hands in mine. When I had first begun to earn a lot of money, I remembered I had also had these conflicting feelings. But I had worked hard for many years to earn what I had, so I deserved to enjoy it. Donating time and money to charity was also important to me, so I continued to do this. That was why the Icon Foundation that Cassie ran was so important to me. To us.

Cassie did not need to feel guilty, but I understood this was still new to her. My priority was to make her happy. If this holiday cost one million pounds I would pay it just to see her smile. That also meant that it was important to give her what she needed if it was something money could not buy.

'So, tell me. What would you like to do? You want to cancel the holiday? Of course, we can do this if you wish and perhaps it is not a bad thing, because like I said before, it is safer not to travel so far—I would prefer if we stayed somewhere near a city. But they will not return the money, so if we do not go, it will go to waste, which is not good.'

'I know. I just checked the contract. I was thinking about it in the car and it wouldn't be fair to change the holiday completely. We've promised everyone a holiday in a nice cabin, which they're looking forward to, so it would be wrong not to honour that. We just don't need all the bells and whistles. So we can still go, but just make it more low-key.'

'How?'

'Do you remember our first Christmas together?'

'Of course.'

'It was just me and you in my little London flat with a tree, some food and films. That's it. And yet it was the best Christmas ever. That's how I'd like this holiday to be. I know we've already ordered the tree and because it's a bit off the beaten track we've got a load of food, but we don't need all the other stuff. We don't need a chef for example.'

'You want to cook three times every day for twelve people?'

'We can all pitch in. That's what normal people do when they go away. And we don't need a team of chauffeurs. I'm sure Mike, Nate, Bella or Lily won't mind driving the hire cars. We can entertain little Leo and Paul ourselves. One of the guys can dress up as Father Christmas. Plus it'll be good practice for us to try and keep the kids entertained.'

'What about the masseuse? Your legs and back hurt often.'

'There's no one's hands I'd rather feel on my body than yours…' Cassie smiled and my dick jerked. I would love to touch her. To ravish every inch of her, but I could not. We had to wait.

'So no chef, no chauffeurs, no masseuse and no entertainers?'

'Yep.'

'And this will make you happy?'

'Yes.' She smiled. 'I'd love to have a simple holiday. No pulling flashy strings, just enjoying normal things and being down to earth. We'll already be staying in a luxury cabin with a fancy tree and have nice food. We don't need anything else. Remember when we first met, you said Christmas shouldn't be about making people feel good by buying big things?'

'I remember. We spoke about this after you gave money to the homeless man.'

'Yep. What you said that night was true. And that's the energy I'd like to channel for this holiday. *Togetherness*. Being with our closest friends will be enough.'

I could not lie. As much as I liked to keep my feet on the ground, I had become used to eating good quality home-cooked meals. And although I liked to cook sometimes, doing this every day for a dozen people was not a challenge that I would choose voluntarily. But Cassie was right. The important thing was spending time with the people we loved.

'If this is what you want, then we will do it.'

'Really? So for the whole holiday you promise we can just keep it simple? Be normal? No "staff", no private planes or extravagance?'

'*Oui.*'

'Promise?'

'You have my word.' I stroked her cheek.

I could do this. I was not born rich. I remembered how life used to be before I had money. It was not that long ago.

Would doing everything ourselves be easy? *Non*.

But I had promised Cassie I would give her the perfect Christmas holiday before our baby arrived and that was exactly what I would do.

3

———

CASSIE

As the order confirmation email pinged in my inbox, I breathed a sigh of relief.

The scary-looking soft toy that Bella said her seven-year-old son, Paul, had his heart set on for Christmas was ordered. So were the Playmobil toys that our friend Sophia said her four-year-old, Leo, adored. Everything was sorted.

In the interest of keeping things simple and low-key, I'd messaged everyone last night to let them know they didn't need to worry about getting presents for me and Nico. We didn't need anything, and the last thing I wanted was them getting themselves into debt just to keep up appearances.

I'd also asked if they minded if we shared the cooking and the driving and thankfully everyone was cool about it.

I knew that they were looking forward to a relaxing holiday and I didn't want them to spend hours in the kitchen every day just because we weren't having a chef, so I'd ordered quick and easy party food from the supermarkets and arranged for it to be delivered directly to the cabin.

And I'd said if everyone let me know their favourite charities, Nico and I would make a donation to them using the money we would've used to pay for the chef, etc.

Hopefully now I'd struck the right balance between giving them the amazing holiday we'd promised and not being too wasteful or extravagant. I was so excited. This trip couldn't come fast enough.

I pulled out my phone and started typing a text.

Me

All set for our trip! Tree, food, drink, decorations and gifts for Paul and Leo ordered. Can't wait to see you guys!

I clicked on the Send button in the group chat, which included the women who were coming on the trip: Bella, who was coming with her husband, Mike, and their son, Paul; my younger sister, Lily, who'd be joined by her boyfriend, Carlos; my other bestie, Melody, who'd be there with my big brother, Nate; and Sophia, who was flying over from Italy, where she lived with her partner, Lorenzo, and little Leo.

Unlike me, Bella, Melody, Lily and Sophia were busy working, so I didn't expect them to reply for now.

My mind drifted to when I used to work in London. Back then, I'd hated my job (well, mainly my boss), but now I absolutely loved my work.

When I'd first visited Nico in Paris, knowing that he loved helping people in need, I'd casually suggested he set up a charitable foundation. You could've knocked me over with a feather when he'd later asked if *I* could run it for him. Of course, I'd accepted.

Being the head of the Icon Foundation meant I spent my days looking for ways to nurture young hairdressing talent and giving people in need a chance to follow their dreams through our hairdressing academy.

I also organised fundraising events for homeless charities. Nico had once lived on the streets himself, so it was a cause that was close to his heart.

Ever since I'd started my role last year, I woke up excited about the day ahead and went to the office with a spring in my step. Work was an important part of my identity, and without it, I felt a bit lost.

But when Nico and I had discussed it, we'd agreed I'd go on maternity leave eight weeks before the birth, then once our little one was six months, I'd go back to work. Mum had only taken off a couple of months when we were all born, so hopefully that amount of leave would be enough.

Speaking of work, maybe I should call the office to check everything was okay. It'd only take a second.

Or I could check the boxes I'd sent last week had been received.

Even before I'd met Nico, I'd always tried to do three good deeds every Christmas, so I'd posted a food and clothing donation package to a homeless charity, a toiletries package to a hygiene poverty charity and a box of new toys to a paediatric hospital.

Just as I was about to hit the dial button, my phoned pinged with a text.

Melody

Sounds fab! What would you like us to bring?

. . .

I quickly typed out a reply.

Me

Just yourselves! Pack warm clothes. Fingers crossed, it'll be snowing!

Me

Oh, and maybe bring some winter boots so we can go for walks.

One of the reasons the accommodation we'd booked was extra popular at Christmas was because it was located in an area where they typically got a lot of snow. And what better way to celebrate the festive season than in a romantic snow-covered cabin?

Having a white Christmas would make everything extra special. We could have snowball fights and make snowmen with Leo and Paul.

I would've loved to go to Lapland, but it wasn't a good idea to fly at this stage of my pregnancy, and with the cabin, we wouldn't have to. It'd be like our own mini winter wonderland. Even without the extras, it was going to be magical.

Melody

I'm so excited! I was showing Andrea the pics of the cabin and she's so jealous. She's regretting not coming now!

Melody

Apart from the chateau for your wedding—oh, and your penthouse—we've never stayed anywhere that's so fancy.

Me

Andrea's still welcome to join us if she likes? There's six bedrooms plus an extra sofa bed, so there's plenty of room.

Melody

Thanks, but she's happy spending Christmas with her mates.

Melody

Blimey! Six bedrooms! I knew it was big, but I didn't realise there'd be that much space!

Me

Yeah, there's also a cinema room, mini bowling alley, our own bar area, Jacuzzi… it's completely kitted out.

Melody

No wonder all the celebs go there!

The luxury set-up was one reason. The fact that there were only two cabins in the whole resort also added to the appeal, because it was more exclusive. Even outside of Christmas, it was popular because the cabins were in a secluded, remote location, so lots of stars went there to escape a scandal or the paparazzi.

Me

Exactly! So the accommodation will be top-notch. You sure you're okay with us taking care of the food ourselves?

Thankfully, I hadn't mentioned anything about the other team of people Nico had suggested hiring.

Melody

Course! Unlike you, Queen Cassie, the rest of us are used to cooking our own food!

As Mum's comments and the words of those women in the café about rich people being out of touch rang in my ears, a sharp pang of guilt shot through my chest.

Me
I still cook too.

That wasn't strictly true. I couldn't remember the last time I had, and that was embarrassing.

Melody
Yeah, right! With your fancy chef, you don't need to worry about food or shopping. Anyway, us normies will make sure we cover the cooking duties! We're already so grateful you invited us to stay somewhere so lovely.

It was just as I thought: Melody believed I wasn't like her anymore. I wasn't a 'normie'. But it'd be fine. I might not cook as much as I used to, but I still remembered how. Once we spent time together, she'd see that even though I had money, I was still the same person.

Bella
Hey, ladies! Just finished a lesson.

Me
Hey!

Melody
Hiya, Bella-boo!

Bella

Cass, don't worry. We're happy to do whatever you need.

Me

Thanks. We won't have to 'cook'—more like just shoving things in the oven, mostly. I've ordered a load of prepared meat joints, party food, nibbles and everything we'll need for the main Christmas meal, so we'll be sorted.

Me

I can boil rice and make pasta, etc., and then for Christmas Day we can all muck in with cooking the turkey. The roast potatoes and veg will already be prepped. Everything we need will be at the cabin when we arrive.

I could've gone all out and ordered food from Harrods, Fortnum & Mason or Selfridges, but M&S and Waitrose were fancy enough for us all. I'd organised some bits from Sainsbury's and Tesco too.

Bella

All sounds perfect! And Mike's happy to drive one of the hire cars from the airport to the cabin.

Melody

Nate said he can drive too.

Me

Amazing! Nico's also up for doing it, so we'll have more than enough drivers to get us to the cabin. I'm so excited!

Bella

Me too! Hon, I've got another lesson now, so I'd better go.

Melody

Same. I've got a shitload of orders to send out before

we leave. Looking forward to seeing you both!
Me
See you in two weeks!

As we signed off with hug emojis and kisses, my heart fluttered. Everything was coming together perfectly. Yes, we might be staying in a posh cabin, but everything else would be nice and low-key.

Lily and Sophia would be fine with the arrangements too, I was sure. I'd double-check with them again later, just in case.

Everyone was going to have a relaxing holiday and I'd get to show my friends and siblings that despite all the money, I was still the same old Cassie. J.Lo's 'Jenny from the Block' would be my anthem. They'd soon see I hadn't forgotten where I'd come from. I'd prove that I wasn't getting too big for my boots or anything like the rich people those women in the café described.

All I needed to do now was make sure Nico didn't mention anything to my friends about us getting a nanny, paying a fortune for me to give birth in a private hospital, or the fact that he'd just shelled out a ridiculous amount of money to buy the entire floor below our penthouse to make room for a nursery, a massive new state-of-the-art master bedroom and a playroom.

Just thinking about it made me wince. My friends were struggling to pay the bills and I was looking at private school brochures, and our baby hadn't even been born yet.

I definitely needed this trip to give my friends the fun, unforgettable Christmas holiday that they deserved.

And to prove that I was still one of them.

4

———

CASSIE

It was finally time for our long-awaited Christmas holiday.

Nico and I had arrived in London yesterday via the Eurostar. We were renting a house here until after the baby was born, so once we'd got settled, we'd gone straight to see Mum and Dad.

If I thought Nico fussed over me, it was nothing compared to my parents. When they weren't cooing over my bump and chatting to it in silly baby language, they were offering me cups of tea every five minutes, propping cushions behind my back or shoving the footstool under my feet.

And of course Mum, who was a big feeder, had cooked enough to feed the five thousand, piling my plate high with my favourite chicken curry and rice, insisting I finished everything seeing as I was *eating for two*.

It was sweet. This would be their first grandchild and they were so excited I expected them to burst.

The funny thing was, it didn't seem like that long ago

that I was still single and sat at the same dining table with my family, and Mum was quizzing me on my romantic prospects and telling me I had to get a move on if I wanted to find a husband and have a baby. And now here I was happily married and pregnant. Just showed how quickly life could change.

It was weird coming back to London and not going to my old flat. I'd only sold it recently. Originally, I'd kept the place as a safety net.

When Nico had asked me to move to Paris to live with him, we'd barely known each other three months. He was France's most eligible billionaire and I was a PA from South London. So on paper, the odds of us going the distance didn't seem great. But we just worked so well together.

Despite all the obstacles—the language barrier, living in another country, missing my family and friends—being with him was so easy. Whenever we were together, all those challenges just faded away.

That was why I'd sold up. I didn't need it anymore. Paris was my home. No—Nico was my home. Wherever he was, that was where I wanted to be.

'Cassandra!' Mum shouted.

This morning we'd returned to my parents'. I'd forgotten to bring their Christmas gifts yesterday, so we thought we'd drop them off before we drove to Scotland.

'Yes, Mum!' I called back from the bathroom. Whenever my mum called me by my full name, I was transported back to being a teenager and feeling like I was in trouble.

'Car's here!'

'Coming!' I flushed the toilet and washed my hands.

Normally, if I was travelling to Scotland to see Dad's maternal side of the family, I would've got the plane. But with less than four weeks to go before I gave birth, I preferred not to fly.

Taking the train would've been okay, but although it'd take longer, we'd decided to travel by car. That way we'd be able to stop off whenever we wanted and I could spread out and put my feet up without other passengers thinking I was a weirdo.

Plus, thanks to the pressure our little bundle of joy was putting on my belly, I'd been farting like a trooper. And put it this way: the air that decided to escape my backside without warning did *not* smell of roses. So I was doing the world a favour by avoiding public transport.

Thankfully Nico was used to my eggy farts and just politely positioned himself by the nearest window when I let one rip.

We'd be meeting everyone at Inverness airport. It was at least an eleven-hour drive, so it wasn't fair to subject them to such a long journey when they could get the plane there in less than a couple of hours.

Once we had all met, we'd drive the hired 4x4s up the mountains to where our cabin was located.

'Don't see why you can't all spend Christmas here with us.' Mum folded her arms as I stepped into the hall-way. Her short silver hair looked elegant as always, and the pink blouse she wore complemented her brown skin perfectly.

'You're going to have a great time!' At least two neigh-bours were having Christmas parties, so if they got bored, Dad said they'd pop in for a tipple or two with them.

'You sure it's safe to travel all that way?'

'Yes, Mum, it'll be fine! I told you. We're having this last holiday as a couple with our best friends before things become full on when the baby arrives. We'll be back down the day after Boxing Day, so we'll be here for New Year's Eve. And remember, we're staying in London for at least six weeks after the birth, to give us time to find our feet before we head back to Paris. So you'll have *plenty* of time to spend with your first grandchild.'

As much as I loved living in Paris, I knew I wanted to give birth in London and have my family and friends around me. Knowing they'd want to see as much of the baby as possible, we'd decided to rent a house in Dulwich for two months to make it easier for everyone to get to.

'Sounds perfect, sweetheart.' Dad squeezed my hand reassuringly. I gave him a quick kiss on the cheek. The salt-and-pepper stubble on his white skin felt prickly against my lips, but I didn't mind.

Mum was so excited that if she had her way, Nico and I and the baby would be living here in the house with them full-time. Never gonna happen, though. We'd drive each other up the wall.

'We should leave,' Nico said softly. 'It is a very long drive and we do not want to arrive too late.'

'Okay.' I picked up my red coat and pea-coloured hat, then headed to the door. 'Let's go.'

The vibration of my phone woke me up. My eyes flashed open. Just as I picked it up, it stopped ringing.

I glanced at the screen. Sophia had called twice.

Wow. I'd been asleep for at least three hours. The last

thing I remembered was stopping off again for the loo and to eat dinner. At that point, we'd been driving for seven hours. Maybe slightly less, because we'd also stopped for lunch and several toilet breaks in between. Either way, that meant there wasn't long until we arrived at the airport.

I looked out the window. The roads and the land beside the motorway were white. It was snowing. *Yes!* Here's hoping it lasted for a few more days.

'*Ça va?*' Nico asked.

'Yeah, good. Just can't believe I slept so long. Sophia's called a few times. I better ring her back.' I dialled her number.

'Hey, Cassie,' Sophia replied, her voice low. She didn't sound like her normal happy self.

'Hi! Everything okay?'

'No, not really. I'm so sorry, but we're not going to make it tonight. We're still in Italy. Lorenzo's having some problems at the restaurant and we need to sort them out before we can come over.'

'Oh no!' My shoulders slumped. 'Sorry to hear that. Is there anything we can help with?'

'No, it's complicated, but thank you.'

'Do you think you'll still be able to make it?' The holiday wouldn't be the same without them.

'Hopefully. Maybe in the next day or so. We'll keep you posted.'

'Okay.'

'Apologies again,' she sighed. I could hear the disappointment and frustration in her voice. I hoped whatever it was wouldn't be too stressful to resolve.

A couple of years ago I would've been worried that my dreaded Christmas curse had struck and that was why they couldn't come today, but it wasn't a disaster. There was still time for them to make it before Christmas.

This was just a teeny tiny setback. The plan was still on track. We'd all be together, just a little later than anticipated.

'It's not your fault! Take care.'

I hung up and filled Nico in on the situation.

'That is a shame. Can we help?'

'I offered, but she said no.'

'Understood. Hopefully they will make it here soon.'

'Speaking of soon, how much longer until we reach the airport?'

'About forty minutes.'

'Great! Just enough time to squeeze in another nap…'

In the end, I didn't sleep. Nico was telling me about an audiobook he'd been listening to, and before we knew it, the driver had pulled up outside the airport. I'd barely stepped out of the car when I heard my name being called.

'Cass!' Melody screamed and ran over to me, her long, striking red hair swooshing from her vibrant purple hat, which stood out against her porcelain skin. 'Bloody hell! You look like you're ready to pop!' She gave me a big squeeze and the sound of her many bangles jangled under her colourful-patterned knitted coat.

'Not quite!' I smiled. 'Still a few weeks to go. Hey, Bella, hi, Lil!' Bella and Lily joined in on the hug. My heart was so full.

Lily and Bella both had light brown skin and dark curly hair. Whereas Bella's hair was in a loose ponytail with a navy wool hat on top which matched her smart long tailored coat, Lily's waves hung loosely above her shoulders. She was wearing a fitted green puffa coat.

'Whoa!' Nate's eyes widened when he saw me. As always, his beard had been shaped to perfection, and his light brown skin glowed like he'd just had a facial. 'Mel's right. You're huge! You sure you're okay to travel when you're so big?'

'Yes, bro!' I rolled my eyes. Nate was just as bad as Nico. 'I wouldn't be going if I wasn't, and they do have hospitals in Scotland, y'know.'

As part of my planning, I'd made a list of the closest ones, so I was fully prepared.

'Very funny.' His eyes narrowed.

'Anyway, the doctor checked me over before I came and everything's fine.'

'Good. I just worry, that's all.'

'*You?* Worry about your sisters? *Never!*' The corner of my mouth twitched.

'You taking the piss?' Nate raised his eyebrow.

'No… well, maybe a little bit. It's sweet that you worry, but like I said, I'm good. And Nico does enough worrying for both of us.' I squeezed Nico's hand affectionately.

'She is not wrong,' Nico smirked.

'Carlos and Mike are already with the 4x4s. Let's go,' Nate commanded, helping Nico take our cases out from the boot.

I wrapped my scarf tighter around my neck, then pulled my hat out of my coat pocket and put it on. My teeth chattered. It was freezing.

We followed Nate, treading carefully through the thick

blanket of snow. The further we got from the airport entrance, the brighter it became: brilliant white, fresh and untouched. I loved the crunching sound it made under my boots as I walked.

A couple of years ago when Nico and I had spent Christmas by the River Thames in London, it had snowed, and I remembered thinking how everything seemed a million times more magical when it had a pretty sprinkling of white flakes. I'd wished for snow and the travel gods had delivered. I was so happy we were going to have a beautiful white Christmas.

As we got closer to the cars, we spotted Carlos and Mike.

Whilst Carlos had olive skin with a hint of dark stubble, jet-black cropped hair and greenish-brown eyes, Mike had dark hair and brown eyes, and his white skin was clean-shaven. They were both wrapped in thick dark winter jackets, jeans and sturdy boots.

Carlos blew into his hands, then rubbed them together. He was from Spain, so probably felt the cold a lot more than the rest of us.

After Nico and I greeted them, Nate loaded everything into the 4x4s.

Nico offered to drive and take Melody and Nate with us, and Mike had volunteered to drive with Bella, Paul, Lily and Carlos. We'd leave the third car we'd hired at the airport for Sophia, Lorenzo and Leo, if they were still able to make it.

As we set off, happy butterflies flooded my chest. It was so great for us all to be together again. The last time was in Provence at my wedding in July, five months ago, and I'd missed them so much.

I hated the thought that we might be growing apart like Mum had suggested, so was looking forward to having the time to catch up face to face. I wanted to hear about *everything*. I didn't want there to be any secrets. If they were worried about something, I wanted to help. That was what real friendship was about. Being there for the lows as well as the highs.

Whilst Melody filled me in on her journey up here, I tried to take in the views. It was difficult to see, though. Once we'd come off the motorway and started driving up the steep mountain, there were no lights to illuminate the narrow road, just the beams from our two cars. And the snow was falling thick and fast.

Although I'd wanted lots of snow, I'd kind of hoped most of it would fall *after* we'd driven up a mountain rather than before, so it wouldn't be so challenging. It'd been a while since Nico had driven too. He hadn't really had much of a need to with Maurice. I hoped we'd be okay.

The higher we climbed, the greater the drop became and the more my heart raced. I wasn't good with heights.

As Nico followed the curve of the road, the car skidded a little. My heart jumped into my mouth.

'The road is very icy,' Nico said.

'How much further is it?' I asked.

'About half an hour.'

'Okay. I might close my eyes for a bit.' If I was sleeping, I wouldn't fret about the roads or tumbling over the mountain's edge. 'You don't mind, do you?' I faced Mel.

'Course not, love. I'll wake you up when we're there.'

What felt like seconds later, rather than thirty minutes, I felt Melody tapping my shoulder gently.

'We're almost here,' she said softly in my ear.'

I blinked quickly, then glanced out of the window. Thick snowflakes landed on the glass. The windscreen wipers were on full blast, but as soon as it cleared away one flurry, another quickly followed. The snow was coming down much harder.

Everything outside looked like it was covered with icing sugar. Now we were near the cabin and close to safety, I was glad the weather forecasters' snowfall predictions were right.

'We have arrived at the resort,' Nico announced. 'The cabin should not be too far away now.'

'Great!' I said enthusiastically.

After that hairy drive up here, I was relieved we wouldn't have to travel back down that slippery mountain until next week. With all the food, drink and other stuff we'd ordered, there was no reason to leave the cabin other than to enjoy the snow right outside our front door or to go for a walk.

It was a good thing too because there wasn't a shop or any other real civilisation for miles, so I knew it was important to be prepared.

A warm feeling flooded my body. It was the satisfaction of knowing that everything was perfectly organised. Despite the concerns I'd had before, everything had worked out and we were going to have the perfect Christmas holiday.

'What's that smell?' Nate said.

'Don't tell me you've let one rip, Cass!' Melody cackled.

'Bloody cheek!' I laughed. 'What's that saying? "Whoever smelt it, dealt it!" And trust me, you'd know if I'd done a bottom burp!'

'Nah.' Nate's voice was solemn. He paused and sniffed the air. 'Smells like something's burning.'

'*Putain de merde!*' Nico shouted.

'What?' I frowned. 'What's happened?'

As he turned on the full beam, my jaw crashed to the floor and my dream of the perfect cosy Christmas in the cabin went up in smoke.

And *smoke* was the right word, because there, in front of us was a scene of total devastation.

There'd been a fire.

Our beautiful cabin, the place I'd dreamed of spending the perfect Christmas holiday in, had burned down.

Shit.

5

———

CASSIE

'Fuck!' Melody shouted as the car drew closer to the cabin.

I took off my seat belt and leant forward to get a better look.

The gorgeous cabin I'd seen in the photos online was now a blackened pile of rubble and ashes.

Instead of seeing the twinkle of brightly coloured Christmas lights adorning the cabin, there were flashing blue lights from the fire engine in front of it and a team of firefighters at the scene.

Bloody hell.

The fire had been put out, but even though the car windows were up, the strong scent of burning filled the air.

Nico pulled over and jumped out, quickly followed by Nate and Melody.

As Mike walked from where he'd parked behind us, I saw concern etched over his face.

But maybe it wasn't our cabin that had burned down. There was still a fifty per cent chance we'd be okay.

Thick smoke billowed from the wreckage. I knew I should stay in the car, but I needed to find out if it really was our cabin that had gone up in flames. God. I hoped no one was in there at the time.

I reached into my handbag, pulled out a mask and quickly covered my face, just to be safe. I was glad I always carried a couple in my bag. Breathing in smoky fumes wouldn't be good for me or the baby.

A small crowd of people had gathered and a policeman was cordoning off the area.

'I hope nobody's hurt.' Bella came up to me.

'That's just what I was thinking. If it's our cabin, it should've been empty from this morning because they needed to prepare it for us, so fingers crossed everyone's safe.'

'I'm glad that at least they've put the fire out,' Melody added.

Nico was on the phone. He ended the call, then headed over to us.

'*Chérie*, you should wait in the car. There is a lot of smoke.'

'I won't stay long. I just wanted to find out what's happening. Was anyone inside? Was that our cabin?'

'I have just spoken to the manager and he is in the hospital.'

'Shit!' I gasped.

'He is okay. They are treating him for the smoke inhalation. And *oui*, he confirmed that this was our cabin.'

'Bollocks!' Melody shouted. 'What are we going to do now?'

'He said the owner is here and has given me his

number,' Nico replied. 'I will call him now to see if they can arrange somewhere for us to stay tonight.'

As Nico dialled the number, we heard ringing a few feet away.

A short, round man, dressed in a tweed jacket, answered.

'Yes, who is this?'

Nico hung up and walked over to him. He must be the owner.

'I am Mr Chevalier. We have a reservation to stay in that cabin for five days—well, the booking is in fact for six nights.'

'Well.' He crossed his arms. 'As you can see, that's not going to happen. The whole thing went up in flames a few hours ago. Which was exactly what I *didn't* need when I'm supposed to be on holiday. Christmas and the New Year are the most profitable time for my cabins and now I'm going to lose a lot of money. God knows how long it'll take to rebuild it and how much it'll cost. Couldn't have happened at a worse time.'

The guy had barely spoken and I already didn't like him. He didn't mention the fact that one of his staff was in hospital because of the fire or show any concern for anyone else's well-being. He was just worried about how much bloody money he was going to lose.

'I am sure that it is very inconvenient for your manager to find himself in hospital just before Christmas too.' Nico ground his jaw. He didn't like this guy either. 'And as for the money, I am sure your insurance will cover that. Do you have another cabin that we can stay in? My wife is heavily pregnant and it is very late, so she needs to rest.'

'No. This is an exclusive resort, so we only have one

other cabin and naturally it's fully booked. Has been for several months. You only got that cabin because there was a cancellation. The customer got an invite to spend Christmas with the royal family instead, so they couldn't pass it up.'

'And our things?' My heart raced. 'We ordered a tree and food and drink and other stuff. Where was that being stored?'

'It was moved into the cabin this afternoon.' He shrugged his shoulders.

'Oh, Cass.' Melody rubbed my back. 'I'm so sorry, love. I know you spent ages organising it all.'

I couldn't believe it had all gone.

Everything.

All those weeks of planning and choosing everything for the perfect Christmas for nothing. I tried to fight back the tears.

My curse was back.

'Don't worry,' Bella said. 'It could've been worse. I don't know what caused the fire, but imagine if we were all in the cabin when it'd happened? At least we're all safe. Things can be replaced. People can't.'

'Yeah,' I sniffed. 'I know. I just wanted everything to be perfect and now it's all ruined.'

'I am sure there is something you can do to help us,' Nico said firmly to the owner.

'I already told you. There isn't. Look, I know you're not short of a few bob. I vet everyone before they stay here. So if I were you, I'd offer the guests in the other cabin a generous incentive to leave and give it to you. They're rich, but not as rich as you, so—'

'*Non!*' Nico said firmly. I could hear the anger in his

voice. That definitely wasn't Nico's style. He'd never kick someone out of their cabin at Christmas. 'That is wrong.'

'*Whatever*. You could try check one of the crappy hotels in town, but I don't rate your chances of finding somewhere else this close to Christmas.'

'Where's your bloody Christmas spirit?' Melody snapped. 'Or your heart? My friend booked this place. I get that you can't help that it burnt down, but you should at least offer us alternative accommodation! She's heavily pregnant for God's sake and it's bloody freezing! What do you expect her to do? Sleep in the snow?'

'My manager deals with that stuff. I only came to check out the damage before I head off to the Maldives. I'm sure you'll work something out,' he said before climbing into his chauffeur-driven 4x4.

'Fucking dickhead,' Nate shouted.

'Forget it,' Nico said. 'We will find another solution.'

'Great.' I sighed. That guy was the kind of self-entitled rich prick I didn't want to end up like. 'Now we're stranded.'

'Do you reckon your assistant knows someone else we could contact to help?' Nate asked.

'It is possible.' Nico paused. Whilst most bosses wouldn't think twice about disturbing their PA whilst they were on holiday, I knew Nico was weighing it up in his mind.

'Reception isn't great here'—Nate looked at his phone —'but I'll see what I can find online first.'

'Me too.' Bella pulled her phone out of her pocket. Fat snowflakes tumbled down from the sky. Several hit her screen and she quickly wiped them away with her thumb.

Mike scooped Paul into his arms and led him back to the car. It was late, so he must be tired.

Whilst Bella and Nate looked for hotels, the emergency services left the scene. Didn't seem like much more they could do, and the snow was coming down thick and fast.

'It's not looking good.' Nate rubbed the back of his neck as he continued scrolling through his phone. 'The nearest town is miles away. There's only two hotels and it says online that they're both fully booked. And it's gonna be hard to find accommodation for nine people. Or twelve depending on when Sophia, Lorenzo and Leo come.'

'It's like being stranded in France all over again,' Melody sighed. 'Like when we were on our way to Cass and Nico's wedding.'

'Yeah. At least there we got the last room. I don't rate our chances this time around. I'll call both hotels now, though, just in case.'

'You call one and I'll call the other,' said Bella.

'Hello, yeah, hi,' said Nate. 'Do you have five rooms available? For tonight? Like, in the next hour? Right. Yeah. Thought so. Thanks.' He ended the call. 'Nope. No luck. Let's see if Bella has any joy.'

'Fully booked,' Bella huffed. 'I've no idea what we're going to do.'

'Looks like we'll have to sleep in the car,' I said.

'If we weren't so tired and it wasn't so late, we could drive to back to the city or something,' Nate suggested.

'The roads were pretty icy on the way up, though.' My heart leapt into my throat at the thought of driving down the mountain again. 'It could be dangerous. Especially with how fast the snow is falling.'

God knows how that arsehole owner was going to get

back down the mountain, or the emergency services, but I'd rather not risk it.

'You are right.' Nico walked over to me and placed a blanket around my shoulders to keep me warm. With all the commotion, I hadn't noticed he'd gone back to the car to get one. 'It is safer to find somewhere nearby.'

'Thanks for the blanket.' I squeezed his hand. 'They've just tried the nearest hotels. From what I remember when I did my research, there's nowhere else for miles.'

Shit. If I hadn't told Nico to cancel the chef, entertainers and masseuse, we could've just shared the hotel rooms he'd booked for them, which were in the next town. We would've had to double up for the night, but we could've worked something out. At least we wouldn't be freezing our arses off in the cold, wondering where we were going to sleep tonight.

Normally between us, we'd be able to find a solution, but this time, I couldn't see a way out of this. Put our lives in danger by trying to drive back to the city or stay in the car and risk freezing to death. We didn't have enough blankets and there was only so long we could leave the heating on in the car before the petrol ran out.

'I will call Miriam. She will understand that this is an emergency and will give me the number of someone to contact.'

I nodded. Given my past, ordinarily I'd be against a boss contacting a PA on holiday. But unlike the 'emergencies' my boss used to bother me with, like when he called at 7 a.m. on a Saturday morning because he couldn't find the caviar I'd ordered, this situation was genuinely urgent. The last thing I wanted was for my friends to get ill.

A gust of frigid wind hit me in the face. Even with the

mask on and the blanket around me, the temperature was still biting.

Nico pulled out his phone.

'Excuse me.' An old man approached us. He had a thick white beard and was wearing an old brown coat. 'I couldn't help but overhear that you were supposed to be staying there for Christmas.' He signalled towards the wreckage that was supposed to be our dream cabin.

'*Oui*, that is correct.' Nico locked his screen.

'Terrible thing to happen,' he said in a soft Scottish accent, then shook his head. 'And I'm guessing that Mr Snooty Boots—the owner didn't offer you anywhere else to stay?'

'Arsehole couldn't get out of here fast enough!' Melody snarled. 'I hope he's gonna give you a refund!'

'He bloody better!' I added. 'But yeah, you're right. We don't have anywhere to stay. Don't suppose you know of anywhere local, do you? We're a bit worried about driving back down to the city, and all of the closest hotels are full booked.'

'I might be able to help, but I'm not sure it will be up to your standards…'

'What do you have in mind?' Nico raised his eyebrow.

'It's not much. It's a cabin about half a mile from here. Belonged to me and my wife. But I haven't been able to stay there since she passed.' He hung his head. 'The place holds too many memories. We used to stay there every Christmas with our daughter and… it's hard to be there on my own. Anyway, it's just sitting empty. There might not be enough bedrooms for all of you, but there's a couple of sofas in the living room. It's yours if you want it.'

'That'd be amazing, thanks!' I said quickly. 'We'll take it!'

'Wait,' Nico jumped in. 'Is it safe? As you can see, my wife is pregnant. It needs to be suitable for her to stay in.'

'My wife always dreamed of turning it into a little B&B, but we never got the chance. It's not the Ritz, which I'm guessing is the kind of place you're used to, and it's been a wee while since it's been cleaned… but it's dry and you'll be warmer and safer there then you will out here. And as you can feel, the temperature has dropped, so the roads will be icy at this time of night. I wouldn't want to be driving in these conditions. It's up to you.'

'I'm sure it's fine!' I said.

Even if it was a bit dusty, we weren't too posh to get our hands dirty.

I knew we'd all come here expecting we were going to be treated to a luxurious break, but I was sure the man was exaggerating about it not being like the Ritz. After all, this was a prestigious area, right?

How bad could it be?

6
___

NICO

We had arrived outside the cabin.

I was not sure about this. We did not know this man and I was concerned about how safe the cabin would be for Cassie to stay in.

If it was old, how could we be sure that the roof would not fall down? And if it had been empty for some time, was there water or electricity?

I turned on the full beam of the car lights. It looked a little better than I had feared. It was a pretty log cabin with an outdoor deck that was covered in a thick blanket of snow.

'It looks like a Christmas postcard!' Cassie beamed.

I nodded. It was true that the outside was pleasing, but it was the condition inside that was most important.

After helping Cassie out of the car, I slipped my arm around her waist. We all walked towards the cabin, the thick coating of crisp untouched snow crunching beneath our boots and large snowflakes pelting down from the sky.

On paper, following a stranger to a dark, disused cabin in a remote area was not sensible. If this was a scene in a horror movie, I would think something bad was about to happen. But I had learned to trust my gut. Sometimes it was wrong, like when I had trusted my old best friend. But most of the time my instincts were right. So far, unlike the owner of the luxury cabin, who was rotten, I sensed that this man was good.

'Here we are.' He turned on his torch, pulled out a key and attempted to open the front door. 'It just needs a little nudge…'

He pushed his shoulder firmly against the door, but it was stuck.

The man tried again. Still no luck.

'Let me help.' Nate squared his shoulders, gripped the large rusty metal handle, then heaved himself against the door. Finally it moved. As he pushed it open, a loud creaking noise pierced the air. This really was like a horror movie.

'Follow me.' The man pointed his torch inside. He led us through the dark hallway, the floor beneath us creaking with every step.

A musty scent hit my nostrils. It smelt like an unpleasant cocktail of old rotting wood, damp and dust.

The man turned into a room then flicked on the light switch.

Mon Dieu.

We were in what looked like a large living room and it was clear that no one had lived here for years.

The wood-panelled walls and high rustic ceilings were impressive, but the curtains and the shelf above the large fireplace were coated with thick dust.

The handle hung from the door like it could fall off at any moment and the lights were flickering violently.

Thick cream sheets which were also coated in dust covered the furniture. From the shape, I assumed that there were sofas underneath.

My nose twitched. I sneezed loudly, then tightened my scarf around my neck before removing my coat and draping it over Cassie's shoulders. Even with the blanket I had given her earlier, she still must be cold.

Cassie's eyes were wide and her mouth hung open for a few moments before she closed it quickly. If she had wanted somewhere without *bells and whistles*, her wish had been granted. This cabin could not be more different to the one that we had booked.

I scanned the room. There was no sign of any radiators.

'Do you have heating?' Puffs of frozen breath escaped my lips. 'It is important that I keep my wife and everyone warm.'

'Aye, but in the living room there's just this fireplace.'

Under different circumstances, that would be romantic and perfect for Christmas. But not this time.

'I see.' My heart raced. Fireplaces or burning wood were not recommended for pregnant women. This was not good. 'And how many bedrooms do you have?'

'Three. But the sofas are quite large. I'm sure a couple of you could fit on them. I'll be back in a moment.' The man approached the door. 'I live in a wee cabin about a hundred metres from here. I'll just pick up a few things for you. Make yourself at home.'

'*Merci,*' I replied as I considered the options available to us. My immediate thought was to make a call. What was the point of having money if I could not use my resources and connections in a time of need? Miriam would help us find somewhere else to stay.

'Fuck.' Nate rubbed his hands together.

'*Chérie.*' I rested my hand on Cassie's back. 'We cannot stay here.'

'I know it's a bit… er, basic, but it-it's… fine!' The pitch of her voice was higher than usual.

'It is cold and dusty.'

Although it was kind of the man to offer us a place to stay and I was grateful, this was not a good environment for the mother of my child to be in.

I wanted to turn back. Return to the city and find alternative accommodation that would be more suitable. I turned to Cassie.

'I know what we agreed, but I am going to call Mir—'

'And do what?' Cassie jumped in. 'I thought about it, and even if she miraculously finds somewhere local, how are we going to get there? The snow is coming down hard and even if I wasn't pregnant, we can't fly anywhere. I know this place isn't exactly Buckingham Palace, but it's dry and safe and once we get the heating going, it'll be warm. I think it's our best option for tonight at least. What do you all think?'

'I don't fancy trying to get back down that mountain.' Lily shuddered.

As much as I did not want to admit it, they were probably right. It was not safe to drive back down in these conditions.

'Staying here does seem like the most sensible option right now.' Bella nodded. 'Maybe we can assess our options in the morning?'

'It might not look like much right now, but it's got

potential,' Cassie added. 'Look at that gorgeous fireplace. It's straight out of a Christmas film.'

'We cannot use it.' I shook my head. 'It is not safe.'

'And look at the large windows and the rustic wooden beams. This place has character. It just needs a bit of spit and polish, that's all.'

'Spit?' My face crumpled.

'She means, it just needs a good clean—to tart it up,' Melody explained. 'If we all muck in, we can probably get this place looking half decent. And let's face it. Our options are pretty limited right now, and like Cass, Bells and Lil said, I'd rather stay here than outside. Or risk skidding off the edge of the mountain by trying to drive back down it.'

'*Sì.*' Carlos nodded.

'We'll need to work out what to do about the bedrooms, though, if there's only three,' Nate added.

'Good point,' Lily said.

'Cassie and Nico can take one bedroom, Mike, Bella and Paul will take the other and… well, I can sleep in here on the sofa with Nate and Melody and Lily can take the last bedroom,' Carlos suggested.

Lily glared at Carlos. She did not seem happy with this suggestion, but I agreed that it was best for the women to have the beds.

'Cool with me,' Nate said.

'So staying here: this is okay with you all?' I asked.

Everyone nodded.

'I'll go and see if there are any cleaning products and make a start in here,' Cassie said.

'It's late and we're all tired, so with the state this place is in, there's no way we're going to get everything done tonight. We should just focus on the areas we need for now. So the bedrooms and the sofa for the boys. We can tackle the rest tomorrow. When the man comes back we can ask if he has any fresh bed sheets. If we pair up and take a room for each of us to tackle, we can get it done,' Melody said.

'Don't worry about the living room,' Nate said. 'Me and Carlos will be fine. Let's just focus on getting the rooms ready for you ladies. And Paul.' He tilted his head in the direction of Paul, who was draped over Mike's shoulder and fast asleep.

'*Bien*,' I agreed.

Just as we were about to look around the cabin and search for something to clean, the room plunged into darkness.

I took my phone from my pocket and tapped the torch button. Everyone did the same and I saw Melody walk to the light switch. She pressed it once, then again. Nothing happened.

'The bulb has blown,' Melody said.

'No shit, Sherlock!' Nate laughed.

'Don't say it…' Melody warned.

'Say what?' Lily asked.

'Nate's about to call me Captain Obvious. Inside joke. Long story.'

'Don't panic, guys!' Cassie said. 'I'm sure the man will have new bulbs. Pretty sure I saw a lamp over there too…' Cassie moved her phone, shining her torch around the room. 'There it is!' She started walking towards the window.

'I will go,' I interrupted. '*S'il te plaît*. Stay here. The floorboards feel very loose. I do not want you to fall or hurt yourself.'

After I switched on the lamp, we investigated the room. Nate pulled off the sheets. Underneath were two large blue tartan check fabric sofas. The stitching had come undone on one of the arms, and on the seat of the sofa to the left, there was a large rip on the fabric, exposing the yellow foam underneath. I wondered how old it was.

There was a scuffed coffee table in front of the sofas, and at the other side of the room was a long oak dining table and set of chairs.

'Let's look for the kitchen and cleaning stuff,' Bella said. Cassie went to follow her.

'*Non.*' I shook my head. 'Sit on the sofa and rest. Perhaps you can stay with Paul and the rest of us will prepare the bedrooms.'

'I want to help!'

'*S'il te plaît,*' I said firmly. Cassie rolled her eyes but did as I asked.

'Special delivery!' The man stepped through the door, clutching a pile of bed linen.

'Lifesaver!' Melody said, taking some from him.

'I see the light bulb has gone. I have some spares somewhere. I'll try and find them in the morning. In the meantime, I'll bring some candles.'

'*Merci,*' I said, hoping the candles would be safe for Cassie. 'What is your name?' I asked.

'Rudolph.'

'Like the reindeer!' Melody smiled. 'Very appropriate for this time of year.' Nate glared at Melody. 'Sorry… I bet you've heard that joke a lot.'

'Once or twice…' He smiled. 'But please, call me Rudy.'

'Rudy, it is very kind of you to let us stay here.' I patted his shoulder gently.

'My pleasure. Couldn't leave you out in the cold. Right. Who fancies a tour?'

All the rooms were on one level. First Rudy took us to a medium-size kitchen. The paint was peeling from the dark blue cupboards. Only a few of them had handles; the rest had clearly fallen off. Cookbooks with curled, yellowing pages rested on the tarnished shelves alongside dusty spice jars.

The sink was chipped and the oven looked like it had been installed in the eighties. Surely it could not be safe to use?

Down the hallway there were two smaller bedrooms on one side and a bathroom and one master bedroom on the other.

As I feared, the rooms were cold, but Rudy had turned on the heating, so I hoped it would start working soon. Until then, I would keep Cassie warm with the blankets Rudy gave us from a tall wooden wardrobe.

This place was not what I would choose for my wife, unborn child and our friends, but it was a roof over our heads and for that I was thankful.

We just had to make it through tonight and tomorrow we would decide what to do next.

7

CASSIE

As I sat on the cold toilet seat and took in the sight of the avocado-coloured bathroom and dated beige tiles, I blew out a breath. Whoever came up with the saying *be careful what you wish for* was right.

I'd said I wanted a simple Christmas with no frills and boy had I got it. With jingle bells on.

I reckon the universe had rubbed its hands with glee when it heard me in Nico's office saying I thought it was best if we made the holiday more *low-key*.

It probably said: 'So Cassie wants basic, eh? She doesn't want her friends to think she's too posh? Hold my eggnog! I've got some festive celebrations to fuck up! Woohoo!'

Or maybe Mum had sent out some sort of Christmas wish, asking for me to be brought back down to earth with a bang because I was getting too big for my boots.

Either way, one thing was clear. My Christmas curse was back—with a vengeance. But this time, it wasn't enough to just mess with me. It wanted all of my nearest and dearest to suffer too.

I suppose it had to up the stakes somehow. It'd already given me two blissful Christmases with Nico, so that hall pass had to run out at some point. And after being sick, injured and dumped multiple times during the festive season, having my holiday cabin burn down was clearly the natural next step.

Although I'd been shocked when I'd first seen the inside of Rudy's cabin, what I'd said when I'd tried to put on a brave face was true. At least we were safe and warmish. We could all sit down and decide what to do at breakfast.

Except breakfast required food. And we didn't have any. Shit. I had to do something to sort out this mess.

After wiping myself and flushing the toilet, I pulled up my knickers and turned on the tap.

Dirty brown water spattered from it. Great. Same thing had happened last night and I'd had to use the hand sanitiser in my handbag instead. Looked like I'd be doing that again today.

Once I'd cleaned my hands, I headed to the living room to find Nico and the others.

It was much warmer in here than yesterday. There was an electric heater in one of the corners. Rudy must have brought that over late last night or earlier this morning.

Melody was scrubbing the top of the fireplace, whilst Bella was sweeping the floor. I grabbed a cloth and the all-purpose cleaning bottle from the coffee table, ready to get stuck in.

'Oh no you don't!' Lily said loudly as she came in the

room, clutching a mop. 'The fumes from these products Rudy gave us are too strong. You need to stay out of here.'

'I can just wear a mask!' I hated the idea of not pulling my weight. It wasn't fair. Like Mum said, she'd cleaned all the way up until she gave birth, so I could too.

'Nope.' Melody shook her head.

'It's been a while since you spent some quality aunty-godson time with Paul.' Bella raised her eyebrow. 'He's in our room.'

Just as I was reluctantly about to leave, Nico, Mike, Nate and Carlos came in.

'Morning, *chérie*.' Nico kissed me on the cheek. 'How did you sleep?'

'Okay, thanks.' Truth be told, my back and legs were killing me more than normal, but I just had to suck it up. 'You?'

'I have slept better…'

That I didn't doubt. The bed was a far cry from what Nico was used to. The mattress was lumpy, and every time we moved, the bed frame creaked loudly.

'Ready?' Nate said.

'*Oui*.' Nico nodded.

'Where are you going?' I asked.

'To get more food,' Mike added. 'Rudy dropped off some tinned food and bread for breakfast, but we're going to see what else we can find.'

'Are you driving?' I asked, looking out the large window.

There was a thick blanket of snow, and large snowflakes tumbled down from the sky. It was like the inside of a snow globe.

'Can't.' Mike shook his head. 'The cars are snowed in.

Even if we cleared it, the roads would be too icy. Rudy's going to show us how to walk to the nearest village.'

'Shit.' My mouth dropped. 'The nearest village is miles away.'

'*Oui*. Six miles.' Nico nodded.

'That'll take ages, especially in this weather!' My chest tightened.

'Don't worry, sis.' Nate rubbed my shoulder. 'There's four of us. We'll be fine. We've got warm clothes and all the right gear for walking in the snow. It'll be an adventure! You just focus on resting.'

'Can I talk to you for a sec?' I signalled to Nico to follow me out of the room. Once we were further up the hallway, I stopped. 'I know what I said before, but maybe we should'—I winced—'pull some of your strings.'

'You are sure?'

'Not really…' I sighed. If this happened to anyone else they'd just have to make the most of it. On one hand I felt bad for caving in so soon, but on the other, I didn't want my friends to suffer.

'Actually… it might be difficult.' Nico rubbed the back of his neck. 'I could hire a helicopter to bring us supplies, but in this weather it could be difficult for it to land. If it was a real emergency, we could consider this, but we do not want people to risk their lives, just so we can have a good dinner.'

'You're right.' I nodded. 'Safety should come first. I just hate the idea of you guys trekking in the snow for miles. You sure it'll be safe?'

'*Oui*. Rudy will be with us. He is experienced with dealing with this weather.'

'Okay.' I blew out a breath.

'We will not return until later this afternoon, so do not wait for us to eat lunch.' Nico kissed me gently on the forehead. 'If the water is brown in the bathroom, let it run for a few minutes.'

'Got it, thanks.'

'*À toute à l'heure.*'

'Yep, see you later. And stay safe,' I said, heading back to the living room.

Once they'd left, I flopped onto the sofa.

'What's up?' Lily frowned.

'Just feeling bad about the guys going all that way to get supplies.'

'*Please.*' Melody rolled her eyes. 'They love all that trekking in the snow alpha male shit.'

'Mike practically had dribble rolling down his chin when Nico asked if he minded coming!' Bella laughed. 'To them, it's an adventure. Men—well, the decent ones—will do anything to feel useful in a crisis. Sounds stereotypical, but it's probably a chance for them to channel their inner caveman. They love the idea of having to go out and "hunt" for food. They'll come home as heroes!'

'Yeah!' Melody cackled. 'Plus, it's an excuse to get away from us gossiping for a few hours!'

'Good point.' My shoulders loosened.

'Anyway, why are you still in here?' Lily glared at me, putting her hands on her hips.

'Okay, okay, I'm going! If you need me, I'll be with Paul.'

∽

Surprisingly, the day went quickly. Paul and I coloured in a Christmas fairground image from one of my colouring books for a couple of hours, then we headed to the living room, where Melody, Lily and Bella had just finished cleaning.

I tried and failed to work out how to use the ancient TV. Paul was fascinated by it and asked why it had a 'big box' stuck to the back of the screen.

And when I tried to operate the DVD player, he was mesmerised, asking if the disc holder was to store a mini Frisbee. Yep. The set-up here was very different to the flatscreen TV he was used to at home.

When I couldn't get the DVD player to work, Paul had asked if he could watch Netflix, but there was no phone reception or internet. I had a whole selection of Christmas films like *The Holiday*, *Elf*, *Trading Places* and *Home Alone* lined up to stream from my phone, so it was a shame we couldn't watch them. We just had to find other ways to pass the time.

The girls had made lunch—a couple of tins of soup and bread that Rudy had kindly given us—then, not surprisingly after all the cleaning, they'd all conked out on the sofas. I'd dozed off too.

When we woke up, the boys were back, looking like they'd just trekked through the Antarctic, clutching armfuls of bags.

They'd been out in the cold for hours, so I made them all cups of tea.

By the time Nico, Mike, Nate and Carlos showered and warmed up, it was time to make dinner and I insisted that I'd cook. I'd done nothing but sit on my arse all day and I wanted to pull my weight.

'Veggie curry and rice okay for everyone?' I asked.

'Yep!' they all confirmed.

After assuring Nico that I was fine to cook, I set about cutting up the veg. I'd missed cooking. I thought back to the days when I used to come round to Bella's to cook, or when Melody and I lived together and I whipped up meals for her and her daughter Andrea.

I went through the cupboards to find a pan. As I pulled it out, the handle came off in my hand. Oops. It was fine. Handles were overrated anyway, right?

When I went to turn the knob on the stove, nothing happened. That was when I realised that only one of the four burners worked. It was cool… that just meant things would take a little longer. Yep. Like I said. Totally fine.

By the time I'd finished cooking, I was surprised no one had started eating bits of the crumbling furniture. Everything took three times as long as it normally would, but despite the challenging environment and limited equipment (and multiple visits from Nico checking I was okay), I finally got it done.

'Dinner's ready!' I shouted, turning off the stove. Carlos, Nate and Nico came to the kitchen to help me carry the pot of rice and bowl of curry to the main room. The spicy scent wafted through the air.

'Smells amazing!' Melody said.

'Let's hope it tastes good too,' I said as everyone started pulling out chairs around the table.

'Bella's just giving Paul a shower, so said to start without them.'

'Okay.' I sat down.

'Mind if I sit here?' Lily walked past the seat next to

Carlos and positioned herself at the opposite end of the table between me and Melody. That was odd.

'Oh, yeah—course,' I replied, wondering why she'd chosen that seat. Carlos frowned, clearly just as confused as I was.

'I still can't get any bloody reception!' Melody held her phone up in the air, then moved it to the left and then the right.

'Same,' Lily added, piling a spoon of rice onto her plate.

Since we'd arrived, we'd all tried to get our phones to work in different rooms around the cabin, without any luck. Maybe it was a good thing. At least we'd be able to switch off and enjoy ourselves instead of constantly staring at our screens.

'I need to know if I've got any orders!' Melody huffed.

'Relax, yeah?' Nate said. 'We're supposed to be on holiday. Even if you've got some, which I'm sure you have, there's nothing you can do about it from here. There's a note on the website that you're closed for Christmas and nothing will get shipped until the new year, so let's just enjoy ourselves.'

Melody scowled at Nate, then looked away.

'It's good to disconnect for a bit,' I said quickly to ease the tension. 'Switch off from emails and social media. This is an adventure!' My voice went up several octaves. 'It's a bit like *The Holiday*.'

'Eh?' Melody frowned.

'Y'know how Cameron Diaz's character moved from her fancy house in LA to Kate Winslet's cosy, simple little English cottage. She didn't have much stuff, but she still had an amazing time, and it'll be the same for us!'

'But wasn't Cameron's character still able to use her mobile phone?'

'Maybe…' My voice trailed off. I'd watched the film a million times and I knew she definitely was, but that wasn't the point. What I was trying to highlight was how much happier she was with a simple life.

'Talking of mobiles, we got reception in the village,' Mike said.

'Great!' I replied, mouth half full with curry. At least it tasted decent, which was a relief.

'I spoke to Lorenzo and Sophia briefly. They're still not sure if they can make it. Sounds like they're dealing with a lot of stuff, but I updated them about what happened and gave them the new location, just in case.'

'Thanks. Such a shame they can't be here.' Everyone nodded in agreement then the room fell silent.

Paul bundled towards the table, taking the seat next to Carlos that Lily had left empty, and as Bella sat next to Mike, he kissed her on the cheek, then squeezed her hand.

I was glad to see that at least one couple seemed happy. I didn't know what was going on, but I was sensing a lot of tension. Something wasn't right with Carlos and Lily. I hadn't seen them in person for a couple of months, but normally they were all over each other.

Nate and Melody could never usually be left alone for more than five minutes before they had their tongues down each other's throats.

And then there was me and Nico. Up until I got pregnant, we'd had so much fun together. Laughing and joking and swinging from the chandeliers at every opportunity.

Don't get me wrong. We were still madly in love and he still made me happy, but these days sometimes I felt more like a helpless child than a woman. Just because I was having a baby, I still wanted to feel desired and sexy. Which was hard to do when your ankles and feet were swollen, your back was hurting and you were tired all of the time, but still.

When we'd all met our soulmates, I thought we'd all be happy. I thought this would be a romantic couples getaway, but as I looked around the table of tight faces and felt the tense atmosphere and stony silence, it was the complete opposite.

With the fire disaster, the trip hadn't got off to the best start, but the cabin looked so much better now. Without the dust, it was easier to see the beauty of the intricate wood carvings around the interior and the beautifully woven colourful rugs, and during the daytime, the views of the glens and breathtaking scenery from the outdoor deck were stunning.

Most importantly, we had food and heat, and we were together and safe.

Yeah, we didn't have a Christmas tree or decorations and all the different board games I'd ordered, but there must still be a way for us to enjoy our time together. I had to find a way to save Christmas and rescue this trip.

'Wine!' I said loudly. 'Anyone want some?' Nico shot me a disapproving look. 'I'm not having any, obviously.' I rolled my eyes.

'I won't say no!' Bella said enthusiastically. I went to push out my chair to go to the kitchen.

'I will go,' Nico said firmly.

Nico returned with two of the bottles they'd bought earlier and poured it into everyone's glasses, then topped mine up with water.

'So how was the trek to the shops? What's the village like?' I said, trying to get the conversation going. Normally whenever we were together, it always flowed easily, but not tonight.

'It was not easy walking through the snow for so long,' Nico replied. 'We were lucky that Rudy showed us the way. If not, we would still be lost.'

'The shops were basic,' Nate added. 'The butcher had fuck all left and the supermarket was more like a corner shop. It didn't have much stuff either. We got what we could, but I don't know what we're gonna do for Christmas Day.'

That makes two of us.

'We still have two full days before then,' Nico said. 'I am sure the snow will clear and we can get to a bigger city. If not, I will look into other options…' He turned to face me and I knew exactly what he was suggesting.

'So what does everyone think?' I asked. 'If the weather's better, should we try and drive down the mountain and find somewhere else to stay?'

'I like it here!' Paul beamed. 'I've never seen so much snow in my life! It's so cool! Can we play in the snow tomorrow, Daddy?'

'Course, son!'

'It's not *so* bad…' Bella added. 'Now it's clean. Like Nico said, maybe we should see whether the snow and ice clear up a bit tomorrow?'

'Yeah,' I agreed.

'Is Santa still coming?' said Paul, concern etched across his face.

Crap. I just remembered—the outfit I'd ordered was with everything else that had gone up in flames. Now what was I going to do? And the gifts! I didn't have anything for the kids.

I'd organised this trip because I'd wanted it to be a memorable Christmas for everyone. But now it was in danger of becoming remembered for all the wrong reasons.

'I'm sure he'll be here!' I said enthusiastically, ignoring Bella and Mike's wide-eyed expressions. I was determined to find a way to make them happy. 'Santa loves the snow. He won't let it stop him.'

Paul beamed. Luckily I'd reassured him. Now I just had to find a way to deliver on my promise.

8
____

CASSIE

Everyone finished their food in record time. After attempting to get them to engage in conversation for about twenty minutes, eventually I gave up.

'I'm going to read this one a story and then I'm off to bed,' Mike said. 'Thanks for the food, Cass.'

'Welcome!' I replied.

'I might try and get some kip too. You staying up?' Nate asked Melody.

'Yeah, you go. I'm not ready to sleep yet.'

'Lily, will you use the bed now?' Carlos asked.

'No,' she replied curtly.

'I can use it until you are ready?'

'Do whatever you want.' She started collecting the plates, then stormed into the kitchen.

Ouch. They'd definitely had a fight.

'I'm going to stay up,' I said to Nico. 'If you're tired, you can turn in too.'

'Okay, *chérie*. Call me if you need anything.'

We made quick work of washing the dishes, then all the ladies headed to the sofas and flopped down.

'So what do you want to do?' I said. 'Try and see if we can get this TV to work?' I doubted the outcome would be different to when I'd tried earlier, but after the atmosphere at dinner, I didn't think anyone was up for talking.

'I think I spotted some popcorn in one of the shopping bags. We could have that, drink more wine and have a girly night!' Melody said. The tightness in my chest loosened.

'And I bought a couple of bottles of Prosecco at the airport,' Bella added, 'so we could drink that too.'

'Great plan!' I said.

After bringing the popcorn, wine, Prosecco and hot chocolate for me, we got comfortable on the sofas.

As I readjusted my position, a loud rumble filled the air.

'Ooops!' I winced. 'Sorry…'

The girls frowned and then, as the strong eggy scent hit their nostrils, they grimaced. Melody fanned the air rapidly.

'Bloody hell, Cass! That's lethal! Smells like nuclear waste!'

'Wow!' Bella choked. 'My eyes are watering.'

'I love you, sis'—Lily pinched her nose—'but you could destroy countries with that. That's not nuclear waste. That's a nuclear bomb!'

'I know, I know. Sorry! It's the hormones and the baby. All the veg in that curry probably didn't help either.'

'I used to suffer from frequent bum trumpets too when I was preggers!' Melody cackled.

'Yeah, it's happened all the way through this pregnancy. And I don't even know when I'm about to let one rip. A couple of months ago I was in an important meeting. I just lifted my arm to point to something on the projector screen and a massive fart shot out! Sounded like I'd swallowed a bloody whoopee cushion! It was so embarrassing!'

'Can't be helped.' Lily smiled. 'I'll just remember to carry a gas mask or clothes peg for my nose whenever I'm near you!'

We all burst out laughing and it was the sweetest sound. I'd never been thankful for my farts, but at least my wind issues had helped loosen the tension. *Quite literally.*

'So…' Bella took a handful of popcorn. 'Apart from Cass's flatulence, how is everyone?'

They'd been so busy earlier cleaning, then making lunch and resting, I'm guessing they hadn't had the chance to catch up properly.

'Glad to get some time off!' Melody said. 'The last few months have been manic.'

'You're doing so well with your jewellery,' Lily said.

As well as working full-time for an office supplies company, Melody made her own jewellery, and in the last few months it'd taken off in a big way. She was now stocked in several shops across London, two department stores in France and a few boutiques in Italy.

'Thanks, love.' Melody blushed. 'It's going great guns. Still can't believe it. Although the giant bags under my eyes do. I'm so tired I can barely remember my own name. I needed this break.'

'You've been burning the candle at both ends, doing the day job and your jewellery. Do you think you'll be ready to take the leap and go full-time soon?' said Bella.

'Well…' She opened the bottle of Prosecco and poured it into the glasses. 'Technically I could go full-time now-ish, but I keep thinking all of it could end tomorrow and then where would I be? I can't wait to get out of that shitty nine-to-five, but at the end of the day, it pays the bills. I have to be careful.'

'But Nate would cover things if you needed help. It won't come to that, though,' I said. 'Your sales are going to keep growing.'

'I hope so. Nate's been a diamond. He's been under-standing about me working late. And the lack of action in the bedroom…'

My eyes widened and Lily's did the same.

'I think they're traumatised whenever you talk about doing the deed with their brother,' Bella said.

Yeah, that and the fact that they *weren't* swinging from the chandeliers. I thought I was the only one.

'Oh sorry!' Melody winced. 'I forget sometimes! But yeah, I do feel bad about him going without. I'm just so tired these days I don't have the energy. And even on the rare occasions I haven't been burning the midnight oil, I don't feel like it. It's like my libido's gone out the window. I don't know what's wrong with me.'

'Everyone goes through phases,' Bella added. 'I doubt many people in relationships are always going at it 24/7 consistently. And like you said, you've been working a lot, so your body's exhausted.'

'True. Either that or it's the perimenopause. My periods aren't as regular as they used to be and I read that lack of libido could be a symptom too. I really hope I get my sexual mojo back soon.' Melody took a large glug of Prosecco.

'You will.' Bella rubbed Melody's shoulder gently.

'At least there's a valid reason for you not doing it!' The words flew from my mouth before I could stop them. I needed to speak to someone before I drove myself mad. 'Nico won't go near me, and although I get tired too, like *a lot*, I'm horny as hell and gagging for it, but he's worried it'll hurt the baby.'

The nail in the coffin was when we'd done it around five months in and there was a small amount of blood afterwards. Just some spotting, and he'd freaked out. The doctor said this happened sometimes. She said it was probably because orgasms and the hormones in semen can cause some cramping and spotting after sex or something. Couldn't remember her exact words. Anyway, she checked me out and even though I was fine, Nico shut down. Said we couldn't risk it.

He always said he'd do anything to make me happy, but despite the reassurance from the doctors, he still wasn't willing to even try again. I wanted to understand why, but to me, it just didn't make sense.

'Some men can't get their head around it.' Bella nodded sympathetically.

'It doesn't matter how much I tell him that the baby's protected in there and he's not going to cause any damage, he just gets so worried. I don't know what to do.'

'Can't you just use your vibrator?' Melody cackled. 'But seriously, if you've talked to him about it, there's not much more you can do. Other than be patient. Maybe he'll come around.'

'But when?! I've only got a few weeks until I have the baby and who's to say whether I'll even be interested then? I might have a shitload of stitches or be exhausted from lack of sleep. Sex has always been an important part of our relationship and I wanted to enjoy these last moments we have as a couple, but instead I'm so frustrated.' I winced, worrying that I sounded bad, but it was how I felt.

'I know you're frustrated,' Bella chipped in, 'but like Mel says, you have to be patient. If the roles were reversed and you weren't in the mood, you'd want Nico to be patient with you too.'

'Yeah.' I grabbed a handful of popcorn. 'You're right.'

'How about you, Lil? You're a bit quiet!' Melody said. 'Trying not to make us feel jealous about you and Carlos going at it like rabbits?'

Lily's face fell.

'What's wrong, Lil?' My face creased. 'I sensed a bit of tension between you two at dinner. You didn't sit next to Carlos and you didn't seem your normal self around him.'

'Come on,' Melody said softly, rubbing Lily's back. 'Whatever it is, you can tell us.'

Lily went to speak, paused, then took a deep breath.

'You're right. Things aren't good.'

'Why? What's up?' I said.

'I think Carlos is having an affair…'

9

———

CASSIE

'What?' Bella gasped.

'No way!' I said.

'*Yes, way*,' Lily replied. 'So I haven't been sleeping with him either. I can't bring myself to do it. I've been worried sick.'

'But what makes you think he's having an affair?' Melody asked.

'The past few weeks he's been acting weird. The last couple of Saturdays he's had to go out *somewhere*. And every time I've offered to come with him, he's said he needed to go by himself. He said it was a *meeting*, but he's never had meetings on Saturday afternoons before.'

'Maybe it's a new club that wants to book him or something,' I suggested. Carlos worked as a DJ and played at top clubs all around the world.

'No. He'd have no reason to be secretive about that. He normally tells me about all his new gigs. And it's not just that. Before, even if I was around, he'd use his phone openly. But now, sometimes when I come in the room, he turns the phone over, or locks the screen and acts shifty. I used to feel really secure, but now, I'm worried he's getting cold feet about the whole relationship with one woman thing.'

Carlos used to live the playboy lifestyle with Nate. The two of them partied hard and enjoyed the ladies for a while, but when Lily had bumped into Carlos during a sabbatical in Spain, they'd started spending time together and ended up falling in love. Since then they'd been insep-arable. Carlos having an affair seemed out of character to me.

'No. Sorry, sis, but I don't buy it. Carlos loves you,' I said.

'Yeah, I still feel like he loves me. He still tries to be affectionate and stuff, but something's off. I can feel it. And I don't think the two are mutually exclusive. You can still love someone and cheat.'

'I'm with Cassie on this one, Lil. I'd put money on him being faithful. Carlos is a good guy and he's not stupid. He knows that if he played away, Nate would chop his dick off!' Melody cackled.

'Good point.' Lily blew out a breath.

'And the rest of us would come after him too!' I smiled.

'Don't worry, Lil.' Bella squeezed her hand. 'There's probably a perfectly good explanation. Talk to him.'

'I want to, but I'm afraid to without real proof. If I accuse him and I'm wrong, that could also damage our relationship.'

'Maybe just ask if everything's okay,' I suggested. 'I'm sure it's innocent.'

'I hope you're right,' Lily said.

'What are we like, eh? I thought we were all blissfully happy, but, Lily, you're fretting about Carlos's commitment, I'm frustrated about Nico wrapping me up in cotton wool and not *servicing* me in the bedroom and, Mel, you've got Nate, who's there, willing, but you haven't felt able to take advantage. *Ugh.* Enough talk about you and my brother banging!'

'I really wish that I could get back to banging your brother. I used to love nothing more than having a ride on his giant cock!'

Melody threw her head back laughing, then froze. I followed her gaze to the living room door where Rudy was standing, his eyes wide. Despite his thick beard, I could still see that his face had turned bright red. He clearly heard *everything* Melody had said.

'I—er, sorry to interrupt,' he stuttered. 'I knocked but I don't think you heard.'

'Please! Come in!' I ushered him in and patted a space on the sofa between me and Melody for him to sit down. 'Would you like some Prosecco?'

'That's very kind, but I won't keep you. I just wanted to check everything was okay with the cabin?'

'Awww, thanks. Yep, we're settling in well. Just having a girls' night.'

'So I heard…' he chuckled.

'Sorry about that, Rudy,' Melody smirked. 'Just relationship stuff… you know.'

'Aye—I do, dear. I was married for forty-nine years.' He let out a deep, infectious laugh. 'But don't worry. All of your problems will pass very soon. And, Melody'— Rudy rested his hand on her shoulder—'I'm sure your wish will be granted. It is Christmas after all. This is a magical time. Everything will work itself out. You'll see… I'll leave you ladies to it.' Rudy smiled, stood up, then headed out to the hallway.

The room fell silent until we heard the loud creak of the front door being pulled shut, confirming that Rudy had left.

'I can't believe he heard me saying I wanted to have a ride on Nate's giant cock!' Melody winced. 'Rudy must be like eighty or something. That's like swearing in front of your grandparents or talking to them about sex. Feels so wrong!'

'Tell that to Doris!' Lily laughed, referring to our friend who was in her late eighties, but was very young at heart.

'Oh yeah! But Doris is a one-off.' Melody repositioned herself in the sofa.

'She is!' I propped my legs up on the coffee table, being careful not to knock over the Prosecco. The baby was kicking and I needed to get comfortable. 'So, Bella-boo, we've all spilled our guts about our problems—please tell us that at least all's well with you and Mike?'

'Thankfully, yes,' Bella replied and we all breathed a collective sigh of relief. 'It's been difficult, financially. Our mortgage payments have shot up and work has been slow. The agencies have been using teachers with less experience because they're cheaper, and more professionals are trying to learn English using free online resources, so there's less money coming in.'

'Shit,' Melody sighed. 'So many people are going through hard times now.'

'Yeah.' Lily nodded.

My heart sank. Complaining about the price of things

and money was one thing we used to do together. Obviously I was relieved I didn't have that issue anymore, but I hated that they were still affected.

'The offer to help still stands if anyone needs it,' I said gently.

'Thanks.' Bella smiled. 'But it'll be fine. I know my mum probably made it sound like we were about to lose our home or something when she was speaking to Aunty Janet, but we're managing. Work should pick up again in the new year, and Mike and I are good.'

'So glad to hear that.' I blew out a breath.

'We've been through worse. Relationships are not easy and it's not all sunshine and rainbows for us either all the time. But you know what they say, without any rain there'd be no flowers. And thankfully, none of our issues are life-threatening or permanent. Everything can be solved. Tomorrow's a new day. I'm sure if you talk to your other halves, you can find a way to work through all of this.'

'Here's hoping,' I said. I couldn't speak for the others, but it wasn't like I hadn't tried voicing my concerns several times to Nico. There wasn't much more I could do other than hope he'd change his mind. But like Bella said, tomorrow was another day.

At least we were all speaking freely, just like we used to. For the rest of the night, I just wanted to enjoy my time with my girlies.

'Now'—I sipped my hot chocolate before picking up their Prosecco—'who wants a top-up?'

10

———

CASSIE

Two more minutes.

I was dying for the loo, but it was so warm and cosy under the blankets I didn't want to move.

Did I say two minutes? At the rate our little munchkin was resting on my bladder, it'd be more like twenty seconds.

Just as I was about to drag my arse out, there was a loud bang.

Nico bolted upright.

'Did you hear that?' he said.

'Yep.'

'Stay here.' He jumped out of the bed. There was just enough sunlight peeping through a gap in the curtains for me to see his naked chest and toned arse in those boxer shorts. *Good Lord.* Yep. The horny hormones were back.

Focus.

I scolded myself. I should be worrying about what that sound was, not thinking about pulling my husband on top of me and making loud banging noises of our own.

After quickly putting on his T-shirt and tracksuit bottoms, Nico gently opened the door and poked his head out. I knew he said I should wait, but I needed to find out what it was. I hobbled out of the bed, grabbed my dressing gown, and when I looked out of the hallway, Bella and Mike were also up and Carlos was walking towards the hallway from the living room.

'What was that noise?' Lily stepped out of her room, rubbing her eyes.

'I checked the kitchen and living room and everything is fine,' Carlos said.

'Sounded like it came from inside the house,' Mike said. 'But if it wasn't in our rooms or the living room, then…'

'The bathroom! The door's closed. It must be in there.' Bella rushed to the door.

'Where's Mel?' I said.

'She's not in the room! Maybe she's in there. She could be hurt! What if she slipped and fell in the shower?' Lily's face crumpled. 'I'm sure I can hear water running.'

'Fuck! You're right,' I said. 'Mel! Are you in there?' We waited several seconds for a response, but there was no answer. 'I'm worried. Can you guys break the door?'

Nico, Carlos and Mike nodded, then stepped back, ready to charge forward.

'After three!' Mike shouted. 'One… two…'

'Wait!' Nate's voice boomed from the other side of the door as it opened slowly.

'Nate? What the hell?' I frowned. 'What's going on?'

'They're going to find out anyway,' I heard Melody huff. 'Might as well get it over with.'

She opened the door and…

OMG!

The sink was detached from the wall. It had collapsed and water was spraying everywhere.

'What the hell happened?' Lily shouted as Nate wrestled to get the water under control.

'I will turn the water off at the mains.' Carlos rushed down the hallway.

'What were you…? Actually'—I waved my hand—'I don't want to know.'

Melody's hair was all over the place, one strap of her nightdress was down and Nate was just in his boxers. It was pretty obvious what they'd been up to…

Bella and Mike erupted into fits of laughter.

'Seriously? In the *sink*?' Lily shook her head.

'We weren't doing it *in* the sink!' Melody protested. 'Just against it. We didn't know it was going to break!'

'We thought you'd all be sleeping.' Nate rubbed the back of his neck. 'It was the only place we could get some privacy. The cars are still snowed in and I wasn't going to start getting it on with my sister in the same room.'

'I'm going back to bed.' Lily shook her head, just as the water finally stopped spraying.

'And I really need to wee, so if you two don't mind leaving… we'll figure out how to fix this later.'

'Sorry, love.' Melody winced.

'It's not all bad…' Bella smirked. I understood what she meant straight away: Melody and Nate were back in the saddle and *connecting* again.

Looked like Rudy was right. Melody had got her wish. I was glad that at least one other couple were starting to enjoy their holiday.

If only I could work out how to get some action from my own husband, things would be peachy.

Just as the thought left my head, I felt a big kick in my stomach. Clearly our little one thought I needed a reminder that they were the most important thing. And that I had another priority to deal with.

Okay, little one. Message received loud and clear.

Time to empty my bladder.

11

NICO

I walked into the living room and smiled. The curtains were open and the whiteness of the snow outside somehow made the room brighter. Although we had not used it, the grand fireplace added character.

When we first arrived, I did not want to stay here. I wanted Cassie and our little treasure to be comfortable and I was not sure that it would be safe. But now, although it was not ideal, this cabin had grown on me. The experience was… humbling.

If Nate and Melody's sink *incident* happened at home, with just one call it would be fixed immediately. Of course it was possible for something to be done here too. Although the plumber could not drive to the cabin, perhaps there were other options.

What I had said to Cassie yesterday about getting supplies was mainly true. It was dangerous to fly and land in this weather. But if we were desperate, perhaps a heli-copter or aircraft could hover in the air and drop supplies to the ground either at the nearest town or close to the cabin.

But the snow was still thick and we were not desperate. We had somewhere safe and warm to stay. It was not worth risking other people's lives just to eat nicer food. And we could manage without a bathroom sink for a day or two.

Despite the tension at dinner, I could also see that everyone, including Cassie, was warming to the cabin. I knew that deep down she still did not want to *pull strings*. It was something that was important to her. So I would honour her original wish. I could already see that she was right. Sometimes it was good to live a simple life. It would make us appreciate our privilege more.

As Nate sat on the sofa and pulled on his boots, I thought about what had happened earlier this morning.

When I realised why he was in the bathroom, I was a little jealous. I had always enjoyed an adventurous sex life with Cassie. We had done many things in bathrooms: making love in the shower, against the wall and even on the cold, tiled floor. But now those escapades were just memories.

Although it would not be appropriate to pin my pregnant wife against a sink and bury myself inside her, that did not mean I no longer had the desire to be intimate.

I pushed those thoughts out of my mind. Our relationship was not just about sex. Our baby was just weeks away from birth: that was the important thing. There were other ways I could make Cassie happy. And I knew one thing that was certain to put a smile on her face.

'You are sure that you do not mind coming with me?' I

said to Mike as he stood beside me at the window and slipped his hands in his gloves.

'Nope. It's an adventure. If it wasn't so far, I'd take Paul with us too. He'd love it.'

'Count us in too,' Nate said, pulling on his hat as Carlos walked towards him, slipping his arms into his jacket.

'*Merci.*'

'Where are you off to?' Cassie walked into the room. She was supposed to be resting in bed.

'We are returning to the village to get something,' I replied.

'Can you get more wine whilst you're there?' Melody called out from the kitchen.

'Yeah, and maybe see if you can pick up a new sink too!' Cassie laughed.

'Oi! I heard that!' Melody shouted.

'Good! That's just the first of many incoming jokes about Bathroomgate!' Cassie grinned. Seeing her smile made my chest expand. That was what I wanted for her every day. I hoped that when we returned I would see that happiness on her face again.

We were going to the village to find a Christmas tree. Cassie had ordered a large one for the cabin with lots of decorations, but of course everything was destroyed in the fire.

I needed to find a replacement. It might not be as good as the one that she had wanted, but I knew that it would not feel like Christmas for her unless we had one.

It was hard to believe that when we had met in London two days before Christmas, Cassie had planned to spend the holidays alone. But after we grew closer, we agreed to spend it together.

I was surprised when she confessed that she did not have a Christmas tree at home. When I heard this, I suggested immediately that we buy one. After we had decorated it, Cassie's face was brighter than the Christmas lights. And watching her smile made me feel so alive. That was when I knew I wanted to dedicate the rest of my life to making her happy. Which was why finding a tree today was so important.

'C'mon.' Nate nodded towards the door. 'We should get going.'

About half an hour into our walk, Nate and Carlos went ahead.

'So'—Mike turned to face me—'that was an interesting wake-up call this morning!'

'*Oui.*' I smiled. As soon as we left the cabin, Nate warned us against making jokes, so I was not surprised that Mike wanted to talk about it. 'Nate is such a confident man who does not normally care about what others think of him, but this morning, he was actually embarrassed!'

'A hundred per cent!' Mike laughed.

'The sink can be fixed. There is no harm. It is not so serious. There is no shame in wanting to satisfy your lady…'

My voice lowered and a sharp pain shot through my chest. I was a hypocrite. I knew that my wife wanted to be satisfied, but I was not listening to her.

I always told Cassie I would do anything for her, but I was not giving her what she needed. Because I was still scarred from my past. Because of my own fears.

Perhaps Mike would understand? He was a father. He

knew what it was like to want to protect your pregnant wife and unborn child from harm. Very few of my friends were fathers. Yes, there was Fabien, and Maurice, but because they were also my employees and worked with Cassie, it did not feel right to speak to them about such personal matters. It would be disrespectful to my wife.

But with Mike, it was different. Just as Cassie I am sure discussed personal things with Bella, I could discuss these matters with him, *non*?

I went to speak and then paused. I did not want to sound stupid. But Mike was kind. He would not laugh at me. And I needed to talk to someone. My temple throbbed. I had bottled up my fears and concerns for months and if I did not express myself, I was worried that my brain might explode.

'Mike. Can I…' This was uncomfortable. I cleared my throat and tried again. 'Do you mind if I ask you something? It is a little… *delicate*.'

Mike raised his eyebrow. 'Course, mate. Whatever you like.'

'*Merci*. When Bella was pregnant, heavily pregnant… as Cassie is now, did you…?' I looked at him, hoping that he would fill in the gap.

'Have sex?'

'*Oui*.' I nodded.

'Yeah. We went through phases. I think most couples do. Sometimes she wasn't interested. Other times she was *very* enthusiastic! I just had to follow her lead, y'know, and roll with it. Be understanding when she wasn't in the mood and, well, be there to provide my, er, *services*, when she needed them. Why? You going through the same thing? It's okay, mate, you can talk to me. It won't go any further.'

I exhaled, grateful that he'd confirmed that I could speak to him in confidence. I took a deep breath.

'Well, Cassie, she… I know she would be happy to make love again, but I am concerned. The last time we tried—a few months ago, there was some blood and I know the doctor said the baby is protected, so in theory I cannot hurt it, but…'

'I get it. I was apprehensive at first too. You feel like a bit of a creep. Sounds dumb, but I used to think that maybe the baby could, y'know, see or feel my dick, but it's not true. Once you get your head around that, things become easier. Cassie's been checked out by your doctor, right?'

'*Oui*. Regularly.'

'Well, if the doctor says she's fine, then I don't think you have anything to worry about. Just take it nice and easy. Check in with her to see that she's okay and comfortable whilst you're doing it, like I'm sure you normally would, and you should be all good.'

'Okay, *merci*.'

'No worries. And if you need to talk more about this stuff and the whole fatherhood thing, I'm here. I've got you.' Mike patted me on the back.

It was strange. I had discussed it with Cassie and with many doctors before and it just always still felt wrong. It still seemed risky. But speaking to Mike helped somehow.

Perhaps I should try again. I pictured Cassie's smile this morning. I had promised myself long ago that I would do anything to make her happy, so as difficult as it was, I needed to ignore my concerns.

The experts had reassured me. Cassie and Mike had

done the same. There was nothing to worry about. Our baby would be fine. This would not be like the last time I had tried with Cassie. And what had happened before, all those years ago, would not happen again.

This time everything would be different.

Oui. It was settled.

If Cassie still wanted this, I would make love to her. Tonight.

12

———

CASSIE

Although every day I felt more comfortable in the cabin, if I stayed inside any longer I'd go crazy. That was why after lunch, me and the girls decided to play outside with Paul.

It felt good to be out in the fresh air. The snow had stopped falling and although it was still inches deep, it wasn't high enough to deter us. If the guys could walk miles in it, we'd be fine playing a few metres outside of our front door.

'Who's up for a snowball fight?' Melody said.

'Me!' Paul said instantly.

'I'm down!' I added.

'You sure?' Bella frowned.

'I'll be fine! Just aim for my legs and obvs avoid the whole belly area…'

'Did you hear that, son? Remember Aunty Cassie has a baby in her tummy, so we have to be very careful.'

'So we don't wake the baby up?' Paul frowned.

'Something like that…'

'How did the baby get into Aunty Cassie's tummy?' Paul looked at Bella. Her face fell.

'Good luck with explaining that!' Melody stifled a laugh.

'Well, um… you see, er…' Bella stuttered. Something told me that she wasn't prepared to have this conversation right now. 'Erm, Uncle Nico had a seed and he planted it inside Aunty Cassie and it grew into a baby inside her tummy. You know like how we plant things in the garden? It's a bit like that.'

'So if I want a baby, I can get my friend to put a seed in my tummy?'

I'd actually thought that Bella's analogy was pretty good, but I should've known Paul wouldn't settle for a simple answer.

'Not quite… only women can grow babies in their tummy.'

'Why?'

'Just because… that's how we're made.'

'So *I* can put a seed in Nisha's tummy?'

'Who's Nisha?' Lily grinned.

'A girl at my school. So, Mummy? Should I ask her if she wants my seed?'

'No! Paul, promise me that you will absolutely *not* ask her that!'

'But why?'

Me, Lily and Melody were seconds away from rolling on the ground laughing. Paul didn't realise how hilarious his words were, bless him. It was so hard to keep a straight face.

'Um, because only adults are allowed to plant seeds in tummies and you and Nisha are far too young. How about

I explain this to you another time? It's a long story and I'm sure you'll get bored. Why don't we build a snowman together instead and then we can have a snowball fight. How does that sound?'

'Cool!'

'Well saved.' I smirked at Bella as she breathed a sigh of relief. I'd love to be a fly on the wall for that *seed and tummy* conversation later…

We took a step back and admired our creation. The snowman looked great. We'd had to improvise and use chocolate biscuits for his eyes and a twig for his nose. I'd sacrificed my hat, which was now happily resting on top of the snowman's head, but my neck was too cold to give up my scarf. I was sure we could find something later to dress him up a bit.

Just as I turned to pick up some more snow, I felt a thud on the back of my leg. I spun around to see Melody grinning.

'Oh, it's on!' I rolled the snow between my gloves, then launched it at her.

Paul joined in the fun, hurling snowballs at his mum and Lily. I bent down slowly to pick up more snow, but felt something on my head.

'Not fair!' I said. 'I gave up my hat for the snowman and you repay me by chucking snow on my hair!' But as I looked up at the others, their eyes were wide.

'Er, Cass… that wasn't snow, love,' Melody said. 'A bird took a fancy to your barnet and er…'

'What?' I put my hand to my head and looked back at

my palm, which was covered in something white and sticky. 'What the hell? I thought birds disappeared for the winter? Did one lone ranger come out of hibernation just to shit on my head? Bloody cheek!'

I went inside, shaking the snow off from my boots and coat.

'I'll get a tissue for your hands,' Bella said.

'Thanks.'

I was about to head to the bathroom to rinse my hair under the sink, but then I remembered. It was broken.

Shit.

Melody and Nate had a lot to answer for.

As inconvenient as it was not having a sink, I bet as far as they were concerned, the sacrifice was worth it. If Nico offered to take me to the bathroom and give me a good seeing-to, I'd be on it like a car bonnet.

I longed for the days when we got it on outside of the bedroom. I'd never forget the first time I visited him in Paris. As I thought about the things we'd got up to on that private river cruise along the Seine and in the car on the way back to the penthouse, goosebumps erupted across my skin.

And then there was the time we had sex on the rooftop. I was certain that Fabien had seen what we got up to.

Last year we'd also got busy in the park and on the private jet. Now *that* was fun. But all that was in the past. Our relationship was entering a new phase. We were no longer carefree adults. We had important responsibilities, which meant we were about to exchange nookie for dirty nappies.

Yep. The days of wild impromptu sex were over.

And the sooner I got used to that, the better.

13

———

NICO

As I walked back to meet Nate and Carlos, my chest tightened and my shoulders felt heavy. We were returning to the cabin without a tree.

I had failed.

When we arrived at the village, we decided to split up. Whilst Nate and Carlos went to the supermarket and butcher's to try and find a turkey for Christmas Day, Mike and I headed to see the man who Rudy said could help us find a tree.

But when we got to his house, he said he had sold the last one earlier this morning, and with the snow still so thick, he claimed he was unable to source more.

Normally, I would not be worried by such a statement. People often said something could not be done. But when you explained that money was not a problem, they miraculously found a way to make things happen. And I was confident that in this situation, if I offered him the right amount, Cassie would have her Christmas tree.

I also knew that if I made just one call, a tree would be

delivered to the cabin, with decorations and whatever Cassie wanted.

Sourcing what was needed would be straightforward, but getting it to the top of a mountain in these weather conditions would not be easy. A suitable place for the private plane or helicopter to land would need to be located. Then a safe path would have to be cleared. It might be challenging, but it was not impossible.

Like I had considered with delivering food supplies, perhaps they could hover in the air and throw the tree to the ground? Then they would not need to land.

Or perhaps I could find a safe way to return to the city that did not involve flying so that we could stay at a proper hotel or rented accommodation. Then everything would be much easier. Finding food, sourcing a tree…

My hand slid into my coat pocket and I reached for my phone. I wanted to make the call. A thirty-second conversation was all it would take. All of our problems would be solved. My finger hovered over the button.

Non.

I could not do it. I had promised Cassie. Despite what she had said, I knew she did not want to pull strings. There would be no *flashiness*. Organising the delivery of a tree would make her happy for a moment. But then when she discovered how it was sourced, she would feel bad. It was not worth it. I would find another way.

When we arrived back to the store, Carlos and Nate were standing outside with their backs to each other and their arms folded.

'Got everything?' Mike asked.

'Not much, but enough to last,' Carlos said.

As we walked back towards the cabin, Nate moved

from Carlos's side and positioned himself next to Mike. That was strange. Normally they were always next to each other, laughing and joking. And during the walk they often went ahead of us, together.

But now I felt tension. They seemed fine earlier, but since we had met up with them again, they had not spoken to each other, which was unusual.

'Is something wrong?' I looked between them.

'Ask *him*.' Nate glared at Carlos.

'It is nothing.' Carlos shook his head.

'Bullshit. If I ask my best mate if he's screwing around and he refuses to answer, I wouldn't call that nothing.'

My eyes widened. Nate was questioning whether Carlos was faithful? That did not sound right.

'No! I told you that is not true!' Carlos's nostrils flared. 'I would not do that to Lily.'

'But you didn't deny that you're keeping secrets from her.'

'That is true, but… I do not want to talk about that right now.'

'Nah, man, that's fucked up. If you can't tell her, at least you can speak to me. I thought we didn't keep secrets?'

'I will talk when the time is right.'

'Can't you see that you're upsetting Lily? I told you when you two got together, if you do anything to hurt my sister, we're done!'

'*Hombre!* You should know me. I love Lily. I would not hurt her.'

'You better not or I'll fucking cut your dick off.'

'Whoa, whoa, whoa!' Mike held his hands up.

'There'll be no dick cutting, okay? It's Christmas. We're on holiday. This is supposed to be a happy time, right?'

'Depends on *him*,' Nate snarled.

'I will explain everything. I promise you. I just need some time to get things clear in my head first, *vale*?'

Nate grunted.

'I am glad this has been resolved.' My shoulders relaxed. 'We have a long walk back to the cabin, so it is better if things are not awkward.'

'Exactly. So, now we've got that out the way, can we finally talk about what happened with the sink this morning…?' Mike smirked and Nate glared.

Looked like that conversation was still off limits…

I was not a person who was afraid of exercise. In Paris, I ran most mornings and regularly worked out in our home gym. But walking for miles in thick snow, carrying heavy bags, was tiring.

Thankfully, we were almost back at the cabin. I could not wait to have a shower. Then I would relax with Cassie. After these long walks I was not sure if I would have the energy to make love tonight. Perhaps tomorrow would be better.

'Finally!' Mike said as we approached the cabin. There was a large snowman at the front, and Lily, Paul and Melody were throwing snowballs. I was glad that Cassie was not outside. The cold would not be good for her and the baby. And throwing snowballs could be dangerous if there was ice inside them.

'Having a snowball fight without me, son?' Mike said.

'Dad!' Paul rushed over and gave him a hug. My heart was full. Mike had such a strong relationship with Paul. He was a great father. I hoped that I would have that same bond with my son or daughter.

'Is Mum inside?'

'Yes. She went to help Aunty Cassie after she had an accident.'

'Accident?' I shouted. I did not wait for Paul to reply. I rushed straight to the cabin.

There was no sign of them in the living room. I heard voices in the kitchen so raced inside and saw Cassie with her head over the sink.

'*Merde!*' I ran to her, my heart thumping through my chest. 'What happened, *chérie*? Are you okay?'

'I'm fine.' She turned to face me. 'Just had a little incident with a bird.'

'*Comment?*' I frowned.

'A bird shat on her head!' Bella laughed.

'It's not funny!' Cassie stifled a smile and my shoulders relaxed.

'That is a relief. I was worried. I thought that it was something serious. Paul said you had an accident.'

'Oh, sorry! He must have mixed up the word *incident* with *accident*. I'm fine. I think it was the bird that had the accident rather than me!' She laughed and my heart grew full again. 'But I'm going to have to wash my hair in the shower. This sink's too small.'

'Come.' I rested my hand on her back. 'I will wash your hair.'

'You sure?'

'Of course.' I took her hand and led her to the bathroom.

As we opened the door and saw the sink on the floor, we both laughed.

'They're never going to live this down!' Cassie said. 'Rudy came round earlier, so we had to tell him. He was cool about it. He disconnected the water supply from the sink somehow and switched the water back on. I said that obviously once the roads were clear, we'd call someone out to fix it and pay to get it replaced.'

'*Bien.* There is a lot that I would like to help him with. The cabin is very beautiful. With some small updates like replacing the kitchen and bathroom and fixing the broken things, perhaps he could fulfil his wife's dream to open this as a small hotel.'

'That would be lovely.'

'So, I was going to have a shower. Perhaps you would like to join me and I can wash your hair at the same time?'

'Oh!' Cassie's eyes widened. 'Yeah! That'd be cool.'

'Wait here. I will get our towels and the products.'

As I stepped into the bedroom, my heart hammered against my chest. I did not know why I was so nervous. We had showered together many times.

I took the shampoo, conditioner and comb out of my suitcase. I always travelled with my hair kit, which included products, scissors and other tools. It was good to be prepared and I also liked cutting hair for the homeless when I had time. I never knew when I would meet somebody in need of a cut or new style.

After getting the towels, I returned to the bathroom and knocked the door.

'Nico?'

'*Oui.*' The door unlocked and I stepped inside.

Mon Dieu.

I swallowed hard as I took in the sight of Cassie. She was completely naked and it was the most beautiful sight I had ever seen.

Cassie's body had always been amazing. I loved every part of her. But now as she stood there, with her ripe stomach, carrying our child, and those full breasts, she had never looked sexier.

'You are…' I did not know if I had the words.

'Fat?'

'*Beautiful*.' I stroked her cheek. 'Breathtaking. Just… incredible. I…' There were no words to describe such exquisiteness.

My dick twitched. Never had I wanted her more. But… I… I needed to wash her hair.

'*Merci*,' Cassie said. 'These boobs are pretty banging, aren't they?' She squeezed them together and I almost exploded in my boxers. 'I wouldn't mind them staying like this forever!' she laughed.

'*Chérie*, your breasts are beautiful whatever size they are. Because they are part of you.'

'Awww, you're so smooth. We're already married, though, and you've already got me knocked up, so no need for the chat-up lines!' She laughed again and my whole body lit up.

I wanted to step forward and suck on those beautiful breasts. I wanted to run my tongue over every inch of her body. But I knew that once I started, I would not be able to stop.

Nate and Melody had already destroyed the sink, but if the circumstances were different, I would want to have Cassie against every part of this room: in the shower, on the floor. Everywhere.

After speaking to Mike, I thought I was ready to try again, but now, I was not so sure. I had to control myself. The shower would be too slippery and the floor tiles too hard and cold. I could not risk hurting her. I just needed to hold on.

Perhaps a few months after the baby was born, if Cassie was healed and felt ready, we could go back to having sex again. Until then, I would continue to restrain myself.

'Come.' I gestured towards the shower. Cassie's face fell and my chest tightened. I had said the wrong thing. And now she felt rejected. *Merde.*

She stepped inside the cubicle and after I removed my clothes, I followed, resting the products and comb on the shelf.

Cassie's gaze travelled over my body, from my face to my shoulders, along my chest and between my legs, where her eyes remained fixated.

As much as I was trying to control myself, there was no way of disguising my erection. I was so hard for her and desperate for relief. I knew that Cassie would be happy to help me, but that would be selfish. If I could not give her pleasure in return, I did not deserve it myself.

At least now she knew that I was still attracted to her.

Very attracted.

I stretched over her, pulling the showerhead from the wall and switching on the water, waiting for it to heat up.

Cassie's gaze lingered on my body and she bit her lip.

This was difficult.

'Perhaps it is better if you turn your back to me and tip your head back, so that the shampoo does not go into your eyes.'

Without saying a word, she turned around, then pushed her bottom against me.

I groaned. She knew what she was doing to me. I squeezed my eyes shut as I ran the warm water over her hair. After reattaching the showerhead, I squeezed the shampoo into my palms and rubbed them together.

As I massaged it gently into Cassie's hair, she rubbed herself against me and moaned.

Mon Dieu.

I had missed the sound of her sweet moans so much.

I continued lathering her hair, my fingers working through her scalp.

'Oh, Nico,' she moaned again, rubbing her hands over her breasts.

My body was in flames. She had no idea how erotic this was. Knowing that massaging her scalp was turning her on, hearing her call my name as she touched herself was making me want her.

Right now, I wanted to lift her up against this wall and bury myself inside her. I was an animal. I should be ashamed.

As I reached for the showerhead again, my body pushed against her back. She shuddered. I squeezed my eyes shut, trying to ignore the burning sensations coursing through my veins, and started rinsing the shampoo from her hair.

'Fuck,' she whimpered. 'You have no idea how good it feels when you touch my scalp.' Her hands continued roaming over her body, then I saw her move her other hand between her legs, before crying out.

I spun her around, to see she'd inserted two fingers into her pussy and was fucking herself.

My chest tightened.

My wife was so frustrated that she had felt that she had no option but to fuck herself when I was right behind her. Not because it was part of foreplay or because she wanted to turn me on, but because she needed to release and knew I wouldn't touch her.

Because I was not doing my job.

My job was to protect her and our baby. But my job was to also keep her satisfied and make her happy.

And I was failing.

This was not right.

Earlier I had told myself that I would try to make love to her again. But instead I had made excuses and done nothing.

I could not continue to neglect my responsibilities. I had to fix this.

'Take out your fingers,' I growled, turning off the shower. 'The only fingers that should be fucking you are mine.'

'But you don't want me.'

'That is not true. Look at me.' I lifted her chin. 'Now, feel this.' I took her hand and placed it on my dick. I needed her to know the effect she had on me. 'I want you so much I feel like I might die. But I am scared.'

'Why?' She ran her hands down my chest. 'I told you, you won't hurt the baby.'

My eyes dropped to the floor. Perhaps if I told her the truth she would understand.

But it was risky.

'Nico?' She rested her hands on my shoulders. 'What is it? Is there something that you're not telling me?'

'*Oui.*' I looked up, and as I saw the concern on her face, my chest tightened.

'Come on. Tell me.'

'Now is not the time. When the baby is born. When I know you are both safe.' I did not want to worry her.

'No! I need to know *now*. I can tell something's up. So if you don't tell me, I'm just going to worry about it even more. *Please.*'

That was true. Like Nate had said to Carlos earlier, keeping secrets from Lily was upsetting her. If I told Cassie now, at least it would be out in the open and we could talk. It would not be easy. But I had hidden this for too long and I could not lie to her.

'Okay.' I slid down to the base of the shower. 'But only if you try to stay calm.'

'Now you're scaring me.'

'Perhaps we should go to the bedroom. Where you will be more comfortable.'

'No! Stop stalling and spit it out!'

I took a deep breath.

'The reason I worry so much… the reason I am scared to make love to you is because…'

This was harder than I thought.

'It's okay,' Cassie said softly. The kindness in her voice gave me the courage to try speaking again.

'It is because, I-I… you are not the only woman that I have got pregnant.'

14

CASSIE

'Wait, what? What the fuck, Nico?' I shouted, my heart thudding against my chest.

Despite the cold drops of water running down my back, my body temperature felt like it had just risen by fifty degrees. 'When you say *I'm not the only woman you've got pregnant*, do you mean there's someone else walking around, carrying your child?'

I slid down slowly to join Nico at the base of the shower, my heart thundering against my chest. I refused to believe that Nico had been with anyone but me since we'd got together. I trusted him. This didn't make sense.

'*Non!*' A look of horror engulfed Nico's face. 'Of course not. I am sorry. Let me explain to you properly: another woman was pregnant with my child, but this happened twenty years ago.'

'Oh!' My heart rate stabilised, but seconds later, it raced again. 'So you have a twenty-year-old son or daughter somewhere? Why didn't you tell me you had a child?'

'Because...' He paused and his face tightened. 'Because, it did not survive.'

'Shit.' I took Nico's hand in mine. 'I'm so sorry. What happened? I mean, you don't have to tell me, but...'

'We were young. We had only been dating for five months. It was not planned, and I admit, when she first told me, I was not happy. I was trying to build my career in Paris. I did not have any money. Neither of us did. We were not ready to be parents, but I wanted to be responsible. Our relationship was always just physical. Even though she was pregnant, she did not show, so we continued to have sex. And once we were close to twelve weeks, we thought everything would be okay. But then...'

Nico stopped talking. I wanted to ask him to continue, but he looked like he needed time to find the words. I squeezed his hand.

'It's okay.'

'Sorry. This is difficult. I have not spoken about this. To anyone.'

'We can stop if you want?'

'But then,' he continued, 'one morning, when I was at work, she called... she was bleeding and had pains. I told her to go to the hospital. I tried to leave the salon as soon as I could, but my boss said I had to stay, and when I got there, the baby was gone. We had lost it.'

'Jesus. That's awful. I'm so sorry.' I threw my arms around him. Nico rested his head on my shoulder.

'The doctors could not explain why it had happened. So I believed it was my fault. That I had done something wrong. Because we had sex that week, I questioned whether it was because I was too rough. If I made her lose the baby.'

'You can't blame yourself. There's so many reasons it could've happened. And I'm sure it had nothing to do with anything either of you did.'

'I will never know for sure.' He pulled away and leant his head against the shower wall. 'But I told myself that if I was ever lucky enough to have the chance to become a father again, I would do everything I could to take care of the mother of my child. That is why I am a little overprotective and worry a lot. And why, after you saw blood when we tried before, I stopped making love to you. I did not want what had happened before to happen again.'

'Oh, darling.' I put my arms around him. 'I wish you'd told me, then I would've understood.'

My heart felt like it had split in two. I was sad that Nico felt he needed to keep this a secret, but I understood why. It was a painful memory. One he didn't want to relive. For him to carry this around for so long must've been awful.

Now so much made sense. His fussing and wanting to make sure I was okay, his keenness to make sure I took things easy, wanting me to give birth in the 'best' hospital and, of course, his fears about being intimate. He'd claimed he was afraid of hurting the baby, but this had seemed so irrational to me that I'd been afraid he'd just stopped wanting me, when really he was suffering in silence and terrified of history repeating itself.

'I am sorry. I did not want to worry you. It is also difficult to talk about. People think that it is only the mother that is affected, which is natural of course. She carries the child and feels everything deeply. But the loss had an impact on me too. Even though at first I said I was not ready, I had started to imagine becoming a father and then that chance was ripped away from me. I found it difficult to process how it could go wrong.'

'I can imagine. Especially because you were young and you didn't have anyone else to talk to. How did it affect your relationship?'

'We broke up soon afterwards. Even if we had not faced such a tragedy, I do not think we would have lasted much longer. But it was too much for either of us to bear. Sometimes I think about what our child would be like now, but it is painful. I must focus on the present. I have been given a second chance to become a father and build a family with the woman I love, and this time I do not want anything bad to happen.'

'This time everything is different.' I took his hands in mine. 'Everything is going to be fine, I can just feel it. Don't worry, okay? I'm strong, I'm healthy, the doctors have been checking me out regularly and our little one is doing great.'

I moved Nico's hand onto my wet stomach. Right on cue our baby kicked. Nico looked up at me. His eyes were red, but when our son or daughter kicked again, his face broke into a smile.

'Feels like you are carrying the next Benzema or Mbappé!'

'They're French football players, right?'

'*Oui.*'

'What makes you think it's a boy? It could be the next Lauren James or Beth Mead!'

'I did not know you were such a big football fan!'

'I'm not, but England's Women's team winning the Euros and reaching the finals of the World Cup was a big deal.'

'I remember.' Nico smiled again.

It was good that he seemed a little bit better. Once our baby was born, perhaps we could speak again about this. See whether he'd consider talking to his therapist, Violette, and working through what had happened.

He'd had therapy before to help him come to terms with his insecurities around his dyslexia and it had worked really well. But for now, it was just important that I was here, ready to give him whatever support he needed. He'd done so much to try and take care of me and now I just wanted to make sure I looked after him too.

'You okay?'

'*Oui.*' He nodded. '*Merci.* For listening and under-standing.'

'That's what I'm here for! And, look, I'm sorry if you felt pressured. We don't have to do anything until after our baby's born and, you know, everything's all good down there again.'

Nico turned to face me, lifted my chin, then kissed me gently.

'*Non.* I am okay. I want to. Cassie, *j'ai envie de toi.* I want you. So much.' We'd been together for years, but the way he said *Cass-seee* in his beautiful accent still made me weak at the knees. 'But it has been a long time and I feel, like… like an animal. I am afraid I will not be able to control myself.'

Hearing that he wanted me made my body tingle.

'I'm happy to try if you're sure? We can take it slow, and if it's painful or anything, we can stop straight away. And you know that sex is actually good for me. So you'd actually be helping me and the baby.'

'How?'

'Every time I have an orgasm it gives my pelvic floor muscles a workout. And I need them for when I go into labour and after the baby's born. Oh, and the stronger my muscles are, the better I can control my need to wee. So in theory, the more I work them out, the less I'll need to get up to go to the loo every night and the better I'll sleep. See? Loads of benefits, but that alone is the perfect reason to get it on, right?' I grinned, wondering if I'd convinced him.

Nico raised his eyebrow suspiciously, paused, then licked his lips.

'Well, if it will help you, this is a good reason to try.'

'And it will help release stress. For both of us. Anyway, I don't want you to feel like you have to. Especially after what you've told me. Just know that whether it's now, next week or after the baby's born and I've healed, if you want me, I'm all yours.'

Nico's eyes darkened. Before I had a chance to continue talking, he crushed his lips onto mine.

Oh. My. God.

Every atom and nerve ending in my body came alive.

It was like my blood had been set on fire.

As his mouth parted, I flicked my tongue against his, running my hands over his broad shoulders, across his chiselled bare chest, then along his abs. And this time when my hand trailed down and reached between his legs, he didn't stop me.

This time when I wrapped my hand around his thick, rock-solid rod, he didn't move it away. Instead, he squeezed his eyes shut and groaned with pleasure.

This time, everything was different.

My pulse quickened.

It was happening.

After months of wanting him, craving him and needing him, my husband was finally about to make love to me.

15

NICO

I took a towel and wrapped it around Cassie. I had not finished washing her hair and I had not showered either, but that would have to wait. Cassie said she wanted me. And I wanted her too.

Telling her about my past and my fears was difficult. I hated keeping that secret from her. Now I had told her everything, I felt lighter. Like a weight had been lifted from my shoulders. Of course, the pain would never go away completely, but I was determined to try and move on from the past.

Cassie was my future—my everything—and I wanted to prove to her how much she meant to me. If that meant facing my fears, I was ready to do it.

After I'd wrapped a towel around my waist, I unlocked the door and checked the hallway was clear. I could not hear anyone in the living room. Everyone must still be outside, playing in the snow.

I picked Cassie up, carried her to our bedroom, then

laid her down. The bed creaked loudly, but I ignored it and locked the door.

As I walked back towards her, I loosened my towel, causing it to drop to the floor. Cassie held her gaze between my legs, then she bit her lip. My dick twitched in response. It was swollen and grew more desperate for relief with every passing second.

I lay down beside her, running my hands over her breasts, then along her stomach. The baby kicked and I almost stopped, then I reminded myself that it was okay.

Everything was going to be fine.

My hands continued travelling downwards until they reached between her thighs. Cassie spread her legs wide as I ran my fingers over her clitoris. Her hips jerked off the bed, causing it to shake.

'Oh God,' she groaned. 'Right there. Please keep touching me.' I stroked and circled her, trying to remain in control. The sight of my beautiful wife with her legs spread for me was something I had missed, and if I was not careful I would come too quickly.

As I continued circling her, need grew within me. Touching her wasn't enough. I wanted to taste her.

I got up, making sure my fingers were still working her the way I knew she liked.

'Can I kiss you?' I asked. '*Here?* It has been too long.'

Fucking Cassie with my mouth was one of my favourite things to do.

'Yes,' she panted. 'It's safe. As long as you don't blow air into me.'

'*Oui*. I remember. Do not worry. I will just lick you.'

I gently parted her lips and ran my tongue over her. As

her juices spilled into my mouth, a guttural sound escaped me. She tasted like heaven.

I continued licking her with long, slow strokes, over and over and over again, growling against her as she pushed herself into me.

'Fuck, Nico!' she screamed, and it was the sweetest sound. I would never get tired of hearing her call my name.

Normally when I feasted on her, I would suck on her clit and graze it with my teeth as I fucked her with my fingers, but today I knew I had to be gentle.

'Tell me what you want,' I said softly.

'I… I need your dick,' she panted. 'Inside me. Now.'

'You are sure?'

'Yes!'

'And you promise that if it is painful or I hurt you, you will tell me to stop?'

'Promise. Quick. Please. I'm so close to coming, but I want you inside me.'

'Would you prefer to go on top, so you can control the pace?'

'No, let's spoon—so with me on my side. That way I won't have to support the weight of my stomach. Just enter me from behind.'

I moved from between her legs and lay behind her. I gripped my dick and lined it up with her entrance. She was so wet, and just knowing how much she wanted this made me want to explode.

I gently slid the first few inches into her and she cried out.

'Are you okay?'

'Yeah! I just forgot how big you are!'

'I can stop and make you come with my mouth instead.'

'No! I want your dick. *All of it.* Considering I'm going to have to push a human out of here in a few weeks, I need a good stretch!' she laughed. 'Give me everything.'

I pushed further into her and growled.

'You feel… this is amazing. I have missed being inside of you.'

'Me too.' She rocked against me, the bed creaking with every movement.

We quickly found our rhythm. It was as if no time had passed. As if she was made for me. As if I had come home.

All of these months I had lived in fear, but now I saw there was no need to be afraid. Our bodies moulded together perfectly, just like they always had.

I reached between her legs again, gently rubbing her clit. I felt her clench around my dick. I knew the signs. She was close. And so was I. After resisting for so long, it was a miracle that I had not come already.

'Harder, please,' she moaned, writhing against me. I thrust into her faster, circling her clit at the same pace.

With every jerk of my hips the bed groaned louder, but I did not care if the others heard us fucking. My wife was about to come and I would not let anything stop me from taking her over the edge.

As her orgasm shattered around her, Cassie screamed loudly.

'Ohhhhh God! Fuuuuck!'

That was my sign to release. A guttural sound flew from my mouth as I exploded inside of her.

Just as I gave one last pump, a sharp cracking sound pierced the air, followed by a loud thud.

The bed frame crumbled beneath us and the mattress sank to the ground. I held on to Cassie tightly, our chests still heaving.

'Oh my God!' Cassie shouted, her breath ragged. 'We just broke the bloody bed!'

'*Oui,*' I replied, still struggling to catch my breath.

'That's a first!' she laughed, and my heart swelled in my chest.

'That is true.' Despite the many places we had made love, I could not remember damaging a single thing. 'But this is not the only thing that has broken in this cabin.' I smiled.

'Oh yeah! First Nate and Mel break the sink and now we've destroyed the bed! Rudy's going to think he's loaned his place to a group of nymphos who are screwing their way around every room!'

'I would understand if he believes this!'

'Wait until Melody and Nate find out! We gave them so much stick about the sink, they'll never let us live this down!'

'I am ready for their jokes,' I laughed. 'I do not care. Breaking the bed was worth it.'

I knew I needed Cassie and to release, but I had not realised how much until now.

Earlier, I said I felt lighter after sharing my secret with her. But now that weightlessness had intensified. It was as if I had been carrying ten thousand stones on my shoulders and they had just been removed.

'Too right!' she chuckled again.

'Is everything good, *chérie*?' The feeling of being inside her was so comforting. I did not want to pull out, but I needed to make sure she was okay.

'Everything is *more* than okay!' she said. Even though her back was still facing me, I could tell that she was smiling. 'Thank you.'

'And how about *mon petit rayon de soleil*?' I gently rested my hand on her stomach. I was relieved to feel some movement.

'Everything is fine with… hold on, let me work out what you called our baby today… your little ray of sunshine?'

'*Exactement!*' I loved when Cassie understood French. It was even sexier when she tried to speak it. 'I will pull out now and bring you a tissue. Just to check that everything is okay.'

'Shame you have to leave,' she sighed as I slid out of her slowly, the mattress still sagging beneath us. 'And don't worry about the tissue. I need to go to the loo anyway.'

'Okay.' I climbed off the bed slowly. The legs attached to the frame closest to the door had given way completely. It was only a matter of time before the two at the head of the bed broke too. 'But let me carry you to the chair. This bed is not safe.'

I carefully scooped Cassie into my arms, picked up the towel that was hanging from the edge of the bed, placed it on the tartan armchair and lowered Cassie into the seat.

'Thanks,' she said, her eyes meeting mine.

Her cheeks were flushed, and as drips of water from her damp hair rolled down her shoulders and over her full breasts, my dick twitched again.

I took in the sight of her gorgeous naked body. That was not an armchair she was sitting on. To me it was a throne. My wife was a goddess. She was my queen. *My everything.*

'Anything else you need?' I knelt beside her and took her hands in mine. I did not know how I had been lucky enough to find such a kind, understanding and sexy woman, but I was grateful that I had.

'No.' Cassie turned to face me and kissed me softly on the lips. 'Just you.'

My heart bloomed inside my chest.

For the first time in months, I truly felt that I had made my wife happy.

And knowing that meant everything.

16

CASSIE

'Have a nice *shower*, did you?' Melody smirked as she walked into the kitchen, where I was buttering a slice of bread. I was starving.

Nico was in the bedroom, setting up everything to do my hair. He'd offered to get the bread for me, but I'd said I was fine to go myself. Nico had already done more than enough for me today…

'Yes, thank you.' The corner of my mouth turned up into a smile.

After I went to the toilet and confirmed that there was no spotting or bleeding, Nico had suggested we finish washing my hair and showering. We got to that… eventually.

Rather than soaping me up, Nico had stroked, then sucked on my nipples before going down on me again, devouring me like he hadn't eaten in months. It was no surprise that my body quickly erupted into yet another orgasm.

I didn't know whether opening up about his past had helped him change his mind about making love to me or if it was something else, but I was just so happy we had. Somehow we felt even closer.

My heart fluttered like it had been invaded by a basket of butterflies. I was walking on air.

'When we came back inside, we heard you screaming and…' Melody paused as Paul wandered into the kitchen. 'And we—we were worried that maybe… the water was too hot.'

Good save.

'Aunty Cassie?' Paul stood in front of me, his face creased. 'Are you okay?'

'I'm good, thanks? You?' I tightened the belt on my dressing gown and readjusted the towel on my head to stop it falling off.

'I'm fine, but we were very worried about you. I came to get a biscuit with Aunty Melody and we heard you screaming. Did the baby hurt you?'

Crap. I'd thought everyone was outside—that was why I hadn't held back. Then again, who was I kidding? It had been so long and the way Nico felt inside of me, I didn't think I would've been able to dial down the volume of my cries of ecstasy even if I tried. At least by the sounds of it, they hadn't heard the bed collapse.

'Um, no, I'm fine. I just…' God, how did you explain away sex noises to a child? Thank God I'd have several years before I had to worry about all that. Just as I was about to repeat Melody's hot water excuse, she jumped in.

'Aunty Cassie wasn't feeling well earlier, but Uncle Nico helped her to feel better, so it's all good now.'

'Oh, okay! It's good that you're better, Aunty. I'm

going back out to play now. Daddy said we can make another snowman!' He ran back outside.

I turned to face Melody and we both burst out laughing.

'Kids, eh?' she said.

'Thanks for saving me!'

'My pleasure! Although, from the sound of your screams earlier, seems like the *pleasure* was all yours! I've heard bloody wild animals make less noise!' Melody cackled.

'*Seriously?*' I raised my eyebrow and smirked. 'You *really* want to go there after what you and my brother got up to this morning?'

'Okay, okay, I walked right into that one! At least you and Nico didn't break anything. Me and Nate are never going to live that down.'

'Actually…' I could probably get away with not telling her, but she'd find out sooner or later. 'We kind of broke the bed…'

'No way!' She gasped. 'I heard it creaking, but you were much louder and I was too busy trying to get Paul back outside to stick around and listen to the whole show! Just how hard were you two fucking?' Melody threw her head back, laughing.

'It wasn't us! It was the old bed. It's been creaking since we got here. It was already on its last legs.'

'And you two thought you'd put it out of its misery by using the power of Nico's *third leg* to finish it off!'

'Stop!' I giggled. It was kind of funny. 'Poor Rudy. He leant us his cabin out of the kindness of his heart and we're destroying it, one piece of furniture at a time.'

'I'm sure he'll understand that we all have *needs*!'

'I'm sure he does after he heard what you said about riding a big dick!' I winced.

'Don't remind me! He seems like a decent bloke, so he wouldn't want us to go without! I'm just happy you got your leg over. Well, I'm happy for the both of us. How was it? How did you manage to persuade Nico that doing it would be safe?'

'We talked and, well, it just kind of happened naturally. And in case you couldn't tell from my screams, it was incredible. So much more intense, it was… *everything*.'

It was true. The orgasms were even more amazing than normal. It was like I was more sensitive down there, which made everything feel deeper and more powerful. It was bloody mind-blowing.

'Probably because it'd been a while. You know what they say: absence makes the heart grow fonder and the cock go wilder!' she cackled.

'Could be! But I reckon it's more than that. It's the connection. Knowing we're having a child together. That we're weeks away from becoming a family. I think that makes everything extra special. Knowing that I'm about to have everything I've ever wanted.'

'I'm so chuffed for you, love.' Melody threw her arms around me. 'I'm glad you have a man to love and support you from the beginning and won't have to go through the shit I did trying to raise a baby on my own.'

'Yeah. I know Andrea's all grown up, but it must be nice having Nate around now.'

'I never thought I'd ever say something about this about your brother, but Nate is the sweetest, kindest, most incredible man I've ever met. And he gets on with Andrea like a house on fire. She loves him to bits. So do I.'

Mel and Nate used to hate each other, but they'd got together at our wedding and had been inseparable ever since. It was nice to see my brother ditching his playboy lifestyle and finally settling down.

'Awww. You're gonna make me cry! I'm so happy for you too, bestie. I know Nate acts like a tough guy, but you can see he loves you both too.'

'Look at us, eh?' Melody took a sip of water. 'All loved up and happy. You, me, Bella… we just need to help Lily and Carlos get back on track.'

'Yeah. I'm sure they'll work it out. Anyway, better get back to Nico.'

'What, for another round?'

'No! He's doing my hair.'

'Is that what the cool kids are calling it now? More like *doing you*!' Melody cackled again.

'It's true!' As much as I'd love to go again, I didn't have it in me. Our *little ray of sunshine* was kicking around happily, my legs were still swollen and my back was hurting.

Yep. Doing my hair was all I'd be doing with Nico today. But there was always tomorrow. Just thinking about it made my body flutter with excitement.

'If you say so, love! Dinner around eight? Bella and Lily are cooking.'

'Sounds great!'

Nico ran the comb gently through the last section of my damp hair, then began to plait it.

'I have almost finished. Are you okay?'

'Yep!'

Nico had prepared a chair with multiple cushions to make me extra comfortable whilst he stood over me and did my hair. There was no mirror nearby, so I couldn't see what he'd done, but I was sure I'd love it. I always did.

My mind drifted back to when Nico had first styled my hair. He'd invited me to Paris, after our Christmas holiday fling. And you could've knocked me over with a feather when he'd asked if I wanted to come to a fancy awards ceremony.

I knew I had to look the part, so had asked if one of his stylists could do my hair as I knew he'd be too busy, but he'd insisted on doing it himself. He'd covered the mirror deliberately so I wouldn't be able to see the results and I was amazed when he did the final reveal, like on one of those makeover shows.

The colour, the cut and style, everything was perfection. That was why he was so successful. I was so lucky that in addition to all of the million other amazing qualities he had, I also had access to his talented hands. He always made me look and feel a billion dollars.

'Finished!' He handed me a mirror.

'I love it!' I admired the four braids he'd plaited close to my scalp.

'*Bien.*'

'Should we go join the others?'

I felt a bit antisocial. Nico and I had been gone for hours and even though I knew everyone had been entertaining themselves outside in the snow, we were still the hosts, so I wanted to make sure everyone was okay.

When we went to the living room, Carlos, Mike and

Nate were playing with Paul, and from the laughter I could hear, I assumed that Melody, Lily and Bella were all in the kitchen.

There was a knock at the door. Shortly afterwards I heard voices in the hallway, then Rudy stepped inside the living room with Melody beside him.

'Evening, everyone.' He smiled.

'Hi!' we replied in unison.

'Your hair looks lovely, dear.' Rudy smiled at me.

'You can thank my hubby for that!'

'You know how to do women's hair?' His eyes widened, clearly impressed.

'Nico's a top hairdresser!' Melody said.

'Oh!' Rudy replied. 'Very good. Can't remember the last time I had a proper haircut. I just use the scissors in the kitchen drawer to give myself a trim.' Everyone gasped. 'I wash them afterwards!' he added quickly.

'I can cut it for you if you would like?' Nico said.

'Oh, no.' Rudy shook his head. 'I couldn't put you to any bother.'

'It would be my pleasure. You have a very impressive head of hair. It is quite unusual to find someone of your, how can I say, of your *vintage*, with such thick, full hair.'

'Thank you.' Rudy blushed. 'My wife always loved my hair. And it's okay, you can call me old! Although I do quite like the term *vintage*!'

'*Bien*. Tell me when you are ready and I will cut it for you.'

'I'll take you up on that. Anyway, could you help me with something? It's outside.' When I looked at Rudy, his gaze dropped to the floor.

'Of course,' Nico replied.

'D'you need us too?' Nate asked.

'No, no. Just young Nicolas.'

'It is a while since somebody has called me young!' Nico laughed before disappearing with Rudy outside.

What was that all about?

17

___

NICO

Cassie was still sleeping when I returned from the bathroom. She looked so peaceful, I did not want to disturb her. I always liked to wake up early. And although we were on holiday, my eyes still opened at the same time.

I had tried to fix the bed last night, but it was beyond repair, so instead, after removing the broken frame and resting the mattress against the wall, I had laid several blankets on the floor, then put the mattress on top. I had also turned the heating up to make sure Cassie did not get cold now that we were sleeping closer to the ground.

After kissing Cassie on her cheek, I leant down and pressed my lips gently on her stomach. I could not believe there were just three weeks until we would finally meet our child.

But first I had to focus on Christmas. Today was Christmas Eve and I still had not found a tree for Cassie. That would change today. I did not care how many kilometres I had to walk. I would make it happen.

When Rudy had come to the house last night, he had

said he might have some news for me this morning. He would be here in ten minutes for me to cut his hair, so I was looking forward to hearing more.

I took my tools to the kitchen. Nate and Carlos were still sleeping in the living room, so I did not want to disturb them. Just as I finished my coffee, I saw Rudy wave at the window, then went to let him in. Once we were in the kitchen, I shut the door, took out my scissors and comb and got to work.

'Did you sleep okay, with just the mattress?' Rudy asked. He was the only one I had told about breaking the bed.

'*Oui, merci.* I will replace everything.'

'It was on its last legs anyway. My wife and I put it to good use over the years.' The corner of his mouth turned up into a smile. 'I'm glad that you and your wife were able to give it a good send-off!'

Rudy's laugh was deep and infectious. I was glad he thought that it was funny.

'We did our best…'

'No bother. And everything will be okay, you know.'

'*Comment?*' I frowned.

'You've been worrying about your wife and if everything will be okay with the baby.'

'*Oui…*' My face crumpled. How did he know this?

'Don't worry.' He reached up to his shoulder where my hand was resting and patted it gently, then moved it away. 'I know that this hasn't been the holiday you planned, but it's Christmas. It'll all work out for you. You'll see.'

'I hope so,' I exhaled. 'Tell me, Rudy, what will you do for Christmas?'

'It's Christmas Eve, so I'll be busy tonight and on

Christmas morning, but after that I'll just make lunch and fall asleep in front of the TV like always.'

'By yourself?'

'Aye. Since my wife passed, it's just been me. My daughter lives in Australia with her husband and my grandson, and air travel is expensive.'

'I see,' I said as I combed through his hair. 'Would you like to spend Christmas here with us?'

Rudy gasped. I could not see his face, but I knew that my suggestion had shocked him.

'I couldn't possibly intrude! The last thing you young 'uns want is to be stuck with an old fart like me.'

'It would be our pleasure. I do not think you should be alone. You are a good man and I know that everyone would be happy for you to join us. And you do not want to make us sad, do you?'

'Course not!' he said before chuckling. 'You're very persuasive. Okay, then. I'd be happy to join you. Thanks very much.'

I continued cutting his hair and then, after getting his permission, began to work on his long, thick white beard. Rudy liked to keep it big, so I promised that I would not touch the length—just neaten it a little.

Fifteen minutes later I was almost done. I just needed to make sure it was perfect. After I had finished with my scissors, I took out my clippers to tidy the back.

Parfait.

'I have finished.' I dusted the hair off from the gown before removing it. 'Would you like to see?'

'Please!'

'Take it.' I gave him a small mirror.

'My goodness!' Rudy's mouth fell open. 'I don't

recognise myself! I look about twenty years younger! I... I don't know how to thank you.'

His lips trembled and his eyes watered. I rested my hand on his shoulder. This happened sometimes. Often when I cut hair for the homeless.

There were people who believed that being a hairdresser was not a valuable or important job. But it was these moments that reminded me of how much hairdressers all over the world were helping people to feel better about themselves every day. Doing this brought me so much joy.

'Your happiness is enough of a gift. And you have already done so much for us. Allowing us to stay here in your beautiful cabin. Please, you must tell me how much you would like us to pay you.'

Rudy waved his hand dismissively.

'I am just happy that it's being used. I haven't been able to step inside it for years without feeling upset, so to hear the laughter and warmth coming from you and your friends makes me happier than you can know.'

'*Merci*, but I must insist. We are using water and electricity. All of these things cost money and I do not feel comfortable letting you cover this.'

I understood that for many older people it could be challenging to cover bills, especially in the current climate. Despite my riches, I still kept up to date with what was happening in the world.

I knew how much the rise in food and energy costs was affecting people. That was why I could not allow Rudy's expenses to increase without covering our share and more. It would not be right.

'Anyway, onto more important things,' Rudy said,

dismissing the conversation. 'The tree. Do you know how to operate a chainsaw?'

'*Comment?*' I frowned.

'A chainsaw—there's a guy a few miles away who's been growing trees, but he's put his back out and can't cut down the last few. If you can get there and chop it down, it's yours. The roads are still bad, though, so you'll need to carry it back.'

'*Fantastique! Merci!* Carrying it will not be a problem. The guys will help. As soon as they are awake, we will go.'

At last, I could provide a tree for Cassie.

It was finally starting to feel like Christmas.

18

CASSIE

When I walked into the living room, Melody and Bella were playing cards and Lily was reading on her Kindle.

'Morning!' I said, as I sat on the sofa. 'Where are the boys?'

'They went on some top-secret trip a couple of hours ago,' said Bella, 'so it's just us. Paul's playing in the bedroom.'

I looked over at Lily, who looked solemn.

'How are you, Lil?'

'Okay.' She shrugged.

'Still haven't worked things out with Carlos?'

Things had still been a bit awkward with them at dinner. They'd disappeared to the bedroom last night, so I'd hoped they'd made up. But from the look on Lily's face, that wasn't the case.

'We spoke.' Lily sighed.

'And?' Melody asked.

'I asked him if everything was okay and he said it was fine and not to worry. But I can't help it.'

'Nate spoke to him too,' Melody said.

'What?' Lily's eyes widened. 'Did you say something to him?'

'No, he just sensed something was up. It's pretty obvious. Anyway, he said he doesn't think Carlos is playing away if that helps. Carlos said he still loves you and he'll talk about whatever it is when the time is right.'

'Oh.' Lily hung her head.

'It'll work itself out.' I squeezed her hand.

There was a loud banging at the door. I attempted to move, but Bella told me to stay on the sofa whilst she and Mel investigated. I heard their voices in the hallway, then they returned.

'Sorry, Cass,' Mel said. 'I'm going to need to blindfold you, love, we have a little surprise.'

'Blindfold me?' The only person that had done that was Nico. The first time was in Paris when he wanted me to try frogs' legs and snails but knew I wouldn't give them a chance if I saw what they looked like. And then after that, well, let's just say that the blindfold was used for more *intimate* things…

'I reckon you'll love this, hon,' Bella reassured me.

'Okay!' My chest fluttered as I wondered what the surprise could be.

Melody left the room, then returned shortly afterwards holding a pair of tights.

'Don't worry, they're clean!' She placed them over my eyes before wrapping them round my head and tying a knot.

Everything went dark and I heard a shuffling sound,

like heavy footsteps coming into the room. There was a loud thump as something hit the floor, followed by a screeching sound which I think was the coffee table being moved.

After what was probably only a few minutes, I felt someone come close to me. It was Nico. I'd recognise his gorgeous woody scent anywhere. My heart fluttered and even our little one started kicking enthusiastically as if it knew that Daddy was close.

The knot behind my head loosened and the tights dropped on my lap. I opened my eyes slowly and…

'Oh my God! You got a tree!' I stood up way too quickly, but I was so happy. 'How? Did you…?'

'*Non.*' Nico shook his head. He knew I was wondering whether he'd pulled strings to get it. 'Rudy told us about someone who grows trees. We cut it down ourselves.'

'Oooh! My sexy lumberjack!' I laughed, then threw my arms around him. 'This is amazing! Thank you!'

'How times change.' Melody smiled. 'If you'd told me a few years ago that you'd get excited about getting a Christmas tree, Cass, I wouldn't have believed you.'

'I know, right?!'

'We still need some decorations, though,' Nate said, putting a box in front of me. 'Rudy gave us this and said to look and see if there's anything you want. It's what his family used years ago.'

'That's so kind of him!' My heart fluttered with excitement.

'We're going back to the village now to see what we can get for Christmas Day.' Nate bent down and gave Melody a soft kiss on the lips. Her whole face lit up.

'Don't you want something to eat or drink first?' I

asked. 'To get your strength up before you start walking millions of miles again? I can make you all a sandwich.'

The guys all looked at each other. They knew it was a good idea. Before Nico could protest or the others offered to help, I went to the kitchen and took the butter and ham out of the fridge. Lily came and helped.

Once the sandwiches were made and they'd all had a hot drink, they set off to the village.

As I walked back into the living room, I felt a twinge in my stomach. I winced and rubbed my belly.

'You okay?' Bella frowned.

'Yeah, just a little throb.' It was more of a cramp than a throb, but it was because I'd moved too quickly.

'Probably the aftermath of Nico's throbbing knob and all your nookie yesterday!' Melody cackled.

'Oh yeah! I heard you and Nico had some *fun* yesterday!' Lily smiled.

'And we heard about the bed…' Bella laughed.

'Sorry! I had to tell them!' Melody chuckled.

'You just wanted to keep the heat off you and Nate!' The corner of my mouth twitched.

'Both of these stories are going to entertain us for years!' Lily added. 'I'm glad things are good between you two again. Aren't you worried, though, about doing it so close to your due date?'

'No, why?'

'Well, doesn't it make the baby come quicker?'

'That's just some old wives' tale.' I waved my hand dismissively. 'There's no real evidence for that.'

'My waters broke when I was hoovering!' Melody said.

'Remind me not to do any hoovering in the next few weeks!'

'Pff,' Melody scoffed. 'Bet you can't remember the last time you did the housework.'

My heart sank. She was right. I hadn't lifted a finger around our home since… probably not since I'd moved to Paris almost two years ago.

'Yeah, you're right. It's bad, isn't it?'

'No!' Melody scoffed. *Oh.* I wasn't expecting *that* to be her reaction. 'It's bloody brilliant. I'd love not to do the housework or cooking.'

'I don't want you to think I'm stuck-up,' I said. 'I'm worried about, y'know… forgetting where I came from. Losing touch with the real world.'

Nico had been brave yesterday when he'd voiced his fears, so it was time I took a leaf out of his book and told my friends about my concerns too.

'No danger of that with us around!' Melody replied.

'It's just, Nico's been talking about nannies and private school and giving birth in a fancy hospital in London and I know it's not because he's being poncy, he's doing it because he wants the best for us, but…'

'You feel like you're selling out?' Bella said.

'Yeah…' My voice trailed off. Her saying that must mean that was what she thought, and that broke my heart.

'Cass…' Bella took both my hands. 'You could never be a sellout if you tried. We know you. Yeah, you might wear more expensive clothes these days and live in a nice penthouse, but you're still *you*. You haven't changed.'

'Thanks.' My chest deflated. Hearing that meant more than she realised. 'I'm not sure you would've thought that if you saw the Christmas celebrations we originally had planned. As well as the chauffeurs and Michelin-starred chef, Nico was going to get a masseuse, babysitter, children's entertainers and all sorts. Could you imagine? When did we ever have a Christmas like that? It was a bit OTT. Mum said I was getting too big for my boots and I didn't want you guys to think I'd gone all la-di-da, so I said I just wanted him to keep things simple.'

'No way!' Melody shouted. 'I'm not gonna lie, those things would've been pretty cool to experience once. And we wouldn't have thought badly of you or Nico. We would've lapped it up!'

'Shit! Sorry.' My face fell. Now I felt like I'd deprived them.

'But you're right,' Melody added. 'The important thing is that we're here together. We don't need that stuff, but enjoying it wouldn't have been wrong either.'

'It all comes down to the reason,' Bella said. 'There's a difference between organising all of those things because you're trying to show off or because we've demanded or expected it. But my guess is that Nico wanted to have those extra things because he wanted to treat us and do everything he could to take care of us. The same for why he wants to organise the private hospital and nanny. He just wants to do right by you and your child. That's his personality. All he wants is to make you happy.'

They were right. A sharp pain hit me again. I rubbed my back.

I knew the guys had offered and even said they enjoyed trekking back and forth in the snow getting supplies, but I knew Nico was holding back from using the resources he had to get the things that we needed because of what I'd said before we arrived about not pulling strings. But really I should just let him do what he thought was best.

If our phones worked, I'd call him right now, suggest they come back and let Nico make the call.

The fact was, Nico was a billionaire. Rather than accepting that, instead I'd been fighting against it.

He'd worked hard for his money, so there was no reason to be ashamed to use it. Especially when we used it to do a lot of good.

Christmas only came once a year, so using some of that cash to treat our closest friends wasn't being flashy. It was showing kindness.

Even though the snow was still thick, it wasn't as bad as when we first arrived, so hopefully we had more options now.

As soon as Nico got back we could make a list of the things everyone wanted and find a way to get everything here in time for tomorrow. From what they'd said about the supplies in the village, I doubted they'd find a turkey. And there was no way I was letting everyone eat soup for Christmas lunch tomorrow.

'You're right, B. Nico's accepted me for who I am and I need to do the same. And seeing as he went to the trouble of getting this tree, I want to make it look pretty by the time he gets back.'

I opened the box of decorations that Nate had given me earlier and rooted through it. There was some red tinsel that had seen better days, silver baubles that were losing their colour and other bits and bobs.

'It's a good start. But I reckon we could make the tree look even better if we made our *own* decorations. You up for it?'

'Count me in!' Lily said.

'Me too!' added Melody.

'Paul will love that. So will I!'

'I'll go and get him.'

As I walked to Paul's bedroom I felt another twinge. *Hmmm.* It felt like a strong period pain. Obviously it couldn't be that, so…

Shit.

What if Lily was right about the sex stimulating labour? No. It was all a myth. I'd read loads of articles and they all said it had no bearing on when you gave birth.

'Fancy making some decorations for the tree?' I looked over at Paul, who was playing on the floor with a dancing milkshake. 'Is that…? You still have it?'

I'd given Paul a dancing milkshake toy a couple of Christmases ago—the same Christmas that I'd met Nico. There was no way I thought he'd still have it, never mind still play with it. I thought kids always got bored of toys quickly.

'It's my favourite!' he said, and my heart swelled. 'What tree are we going to decorate? One of the ones outside in the snow?'

'No, we have a proper Christmas tree! It's in the living room.'

'Cool!' He jumped up and took my hand and I led him to take a look. 'Wow!' His eyes lit up when he saw it.

He ran over to the box and started pulling out the decorations. We all got stuck in, adding the baubles and other trinkets to the branches. There wasn't a lot of stuff in the box, but every little helped.

'Do you have any coloured paper or card, Paul?' I asked.

'Yes! Lots! I'll go and get some.'

'And we need glue!'

'I have some in my little jewellery kit,' said Melody. 'I'll get some scissors from the kitchen. We can make tinfoil ornaments too. We can draw circles on the card, cut them out, cover them with foil, use Paul's colouring pens to decorate them and then all we'll need is some string to hang them on the tree.'

'Perfect!'

The next couple of hours were so much fun. We found an old cassette player in Rudy's box with a Christmas songs tape inside, so we sang along to Wham's 'Last Christmas', Band Aid's 'Do They Know It's Christmas?', 'Rockin' Around the Christmas Tree' and other classics whilst we made a load of decorations.

As well as creating paper chains and tinfoil ornaments, Bella got some pine cones and decorated those and Melody and Lily suggested we make popcorn garlands.

Melody had some jewellery beads and string in her suitcase, so she threaded the beads and some popcorn onto some string.

The old cardboard loo rolls were also perfect for making a few crackers, which we filled with Quality Street chocolates that Bella had bought.

We placed the last items on the tree, then stood back to admire our handiwork.

'It looks so cool!' Paul beamed.

'It really does, son.' Bella kissed Paul on his head.

'We did a brilliant job!' I smiled. This was a million times better than what I'd originally planned. Now that I thought about it, if we'd had expensive decorations, everyone would've been on edge worrying about the cost if one of the kids broke something. 'It's just missing one thing…'

'What is it, Aunty?' Paul frowned.

I rooted around in the box. Pretty sure I'd seen it in here earlier. There it was.

'Now for *la pièce de la résistance*!' I pulled out the angel.

'Wow!' Paul's eyes widened.

After going on tiptoe, I tried to place it on the top of the tree.

'Can you reach?' Lily said. 'Bella could do it. She's the tallest.'

'Thanks, but I've got this.'

I stretched up as high as I could, and as I did a sharp cramping pain shot through my stomach. The twinges had been on and off since this morning. I'd done my best to put on a brave face and continue, but this one was stronger.

'Shit,' I shouted. 'Sorry, Paul.'

'You okay?' Bella asked.

'I'm not sure…' I clutched my belly. 'Don't freak out, but it kind of feels like I'm having… contractions.'

'What!' Lily said.

'Oh my God, sit down!' Melody led me back to the sofa. 'Er, anyone know what to do?'

'What does it feel like?' said Bella. 'Can you describe it?'

'Earlier it was a bit like cramps or really bad period pains. Now it…' I took a deep breath. 'It's like my muscles are tightening, and when they do, it's painful for a bit and then it goes away.'

'That sounds about right…' Bella's voice trailed off. 'Don't fret, though. Might just be Braxton Hicks.'

'And if it's not?' Lily added.

Melody glared at her.

My heart raced. I really hoped it was just a false alarm. Nico wasn't here. I really needed Nico. I couldn't do this without him. I didn't want to.

'Everyone stay calm. Even if Cass is going into labour, the baby isn't going to suddenly pop out in five minutes. It could be several hours, a day or even longer. We should time the contractions to see how often they're happening. Do you have your midwife or doctor's details here?'

'It's in my phone—on the bedside table.'

Lily got up and ran to the bedroom.

'Mel, do you have reception on your phone?' Bella asked.

'Nope.' Melody held her phone up in the air. 'Haven't since we arrived. But Nate said their phones work in the village—that's the only way he's been able to check on Andrea. It's just up here that we don't seem to have a signal.'

Lily returned to the room and handed me my phone. I had zero bars. When we'd arrived and we didn't have reception, it didn't seem like so big of a deal. It was a good way for us to disconnect. Switch off from emails and social media. But now I was starting to realise how essential it was.

Given that I was heavily pregnant, I wouldn't have deliberately chosen to come somewhere without Wi-Fi and phone reception. The cabin we were supposed to rent had all the mod cons and a good internet connection. I wasn't to know that the bloody place was going to burn down and result in us staying somewhere that was cut off from the rest of the world.

'Do you think Rudy has a phone? Like a house phone?' Lily said.

'Worth a try!' Melody said.

'While you find the details, I'll quickly go over and check.' She jumped up and then I heard the door slam behind her.

'I was just thinking: the cabin we were supposed to stay in had Wi-Fi, so if Rudy doesn't have a phone, we could go back there and see if whoever's renting the other cabin would let us use their phone?' I said.

'Good thinking, Batman!' Melody replied.

'Aunty Cassie, what's wrong?' Paul asked.

In all the commotion, I'd forgotten he was here. I hoped I hadn't scared him.

'I'm just not feeling very well right now, sweetheart, but I'll be okay.'

'Should I try and find Uncle Nico so he can make you feel better like yesterday?'

Melody snorted and the corner of my mouth twitched as I remembered our conversation in the kitchen after Nico and I had *showered*.

'That's how she got into this situation nine months ago!' Melody said quietly, trying to stifle a laugh.

'It's okay,' I said. 'He'll be back soon and he can help me th—ouch!' I cried out and gripped my stomach, which felt harder than usual.

'I think that's about eight minutes?' Bella looked at her watch. 'Right now you're good, but let's see when the next one comes.'

As Bella rubbed my back, I took deep breaths. In. Out. In. Out.

Eventually the pain faded. I grabbed a cushion from the sofa, placed it behind me and tried to sit up straighter.

'You okay?' Melody asked.

'For now…'

'Would you like to play with my toys? Or read one of my books?' Paul asked. He was such a sweetie.

'What I'd really love is a glass of water. Do you think you could get me one?'

'Yes!' He rushed off to the kitchen.

I kept on breathing deeply and telling myself to stay calm. Like Bella said, it could be hours until anything happened, if at all, and apart from the intermittent cramping I was fine. It wasn't like my waters had broken or anything. *That* would be a reason to worry.

After picking up my phone, I scrolled through to the Notes app, where I had everything written down in preparation for the birth. All the key contact details and information, just in case.

'Here's the details for the midwife and doctor.' I handed the phone to Bella and she studied the screen. 'I've also got a list of hospitals.'

'Great. Hopefully Lily will be back soon with good news about a phone.'

A few minutes later, Lily rushed back into the living room. Her hat and coat were covered with sleet.

'So the good news is Rudy has a house phone.'

'Oh, thank fuck!' I said, my shoulders loosening.

'I tried calling Nate but there was no answer. Same for Carlos, Nico and Mike. Rudy called the butcher and the supermarket and neither of the owners had seen them come into their shops yet.'

'Shit! What if something's happened to them!' I jumped up off the sofa, my heart thudding.

'Don't worry!' Lily put her arm around me. 'I'm sure they're fine. Rudy reckons that if they left about an hour and forty-five minutes ago, they probably haven't arrived yet. It takes at least two hours to walk there.'

'I need to do something!' I grabbed my phone and hobbled over to the window to check if miraculously there would be some reception.

'The best thing you can do is just rest—come and sit back down,' Bella said.

Paul returned, clutching a glass of water. He handed it to me, beaming proudly.

'Thanks! You're so helpful!' I took several gulps.

'I'm going to get something else for you now!' Paul said.

I walked a few steps towards the sofa, then stopped and held my phone up in the air again. I didn't know why I thought the availability of reception would've changed, but it was worth a try.

My phone slipped out of my hand and fell onto the floor. Thank God I had a decent case so it'd be protected. I bent down to pick it up and heard a pop. I must've bent down too quickly.

'So I think we should maybe see if you have any more contractions in the next hour and then we can decide whether or not to call the midwife.'

'Ha! That's the name of that TV show!' Melody laughed.

'Isn't it best to do it sooner rather than later?' Lily asked.

'I'm not sure. Cass has only had a few so far and

they're not too close together yet. We need to see if they're consistent,' Bella replied.

Paul came back in the room, clutching what looked like the dancing milkshake in his hands. He started walking towards me, then stopped in his tracks.

'Aunty Cassie, did you spill your water? Do you want me to get you another glass?'

'Huh?' I frowned, looking down at the wooden floor.

What the hell?

As I followed Paul's gaze, I saw there was water on the floor beneath me. Then I felt a slow trickle rolling down my inner thigh. My knickers were also damp.

Either I'd wet myself or my waters had just broken.

Something told me the dampness had nothing to do with wee.

Which meant the baby was coming.

Shit.

As we walked through the snow, I felt calm. Today I was a different man. My shoulders were lighter than they had been when we had come to the village yesterday and my chest did not seem as tight.

It was clear. I had worried too much. I saw that now. Cassie was right. No harm had come to the baby and she was fine. If I had known before that making love to her again would have been so free of trouble and complications, I would have done it sooner. But I could not change the past. The important thing was that now we were good again.

A wave of happiness filled my stomach as I thought back to all of the things we had done together after the shower. Being with Cassie was always special, but somehow I felt even more connected. Knowing that she was carrying our child, that her body was going through all of these wonderful changes that would result in me becoming a father, was beautiful.

'You alright there, mate?' Mike looked at me.

'*Oui.*' My face broke into a smile. 'I am good. *Very good…*'

I wanted to elaborate and to thank him, because without Mike's words of encouragement, perhaps I would not have had the courage to speak to Cassie and try again. But Nate was here and I felt uncomfortable discussing what I had done with his sister last night. And I knew that he would feel the same.

'I am ready to talk,' Carlos said to Nate. 'I want to share what has been on my mind.'

'Oh.' Nate raised his eyebrow. 'Cool.'

'But you must promise to keep it to yourself.' Carlos looked at me.

'It is okay—you can walk ahead,' I replied. I understood that it was something private and whilst they discussed it, I could talk to Mike.

Mike and I stopped in the snow and allowed them to carry on. We knew the route to the village now, so I was not concerned that we would get lost. Once they were out of sight, we continued.

'So you going to tell me what's responsible for that big grin you've had plastered on your face all morning? Something tells me it's not just because you're excited about Christmas Day tomorrow.' Mike smirked.

'Cassie. We… yesterday, things *happened.*'

'Nice! I'm happy for you. And I'm guessing everything was okay afterwards?'

'*Oui.* Everything was perfect. Well, the bed broke, but…'

'No way!' Mike chuckled. 'I'm starting to feel left out! Maybe Bella and I should try and break the sofa later!'

'Perhaps Rudy will ask us to leave if we break something else!' I laughed. 'Anyway, Cassie is happy and the baby is fine. She did not see any problems, so I wanted to say *merci beaucoup*. Your advice helped a lot. I am very grateful.'

'No worries. I'm just glad you're back on track.'

'I am too.'

'So do you reckon we'll find a turkey in the village?'

'I think it is unlikely,' I sighed. 'But do not worry. When we get back to the cabin I will speak to Cassie. It will be simple for me to solve these problems. I have people I can call to help.'

'Do you want to call them in the village? I'm going to call Lorenzo and Sophia again to see if they think they'll still make it and I know Nate wanted to check on Andrea. Reception is bad at the cabin. Well, worse than bad—non-existent.'

'True. But I remember there was reception at the cabin where we were supposed to stay. Nate and Bella were able to make calls there. It is not too far to walk. I promised Cassie that I would try to live a simple life during this holiday, but I am confident that when she discovers that we will not have food for a proper Christmas dinner, she will change her mind.'

We saw Carlos and Nate in the distance. They had stopped and were waiting for us. As we got closer, they were both smiling.

'You two look much happier!' Mike patted Carlos on the back. 'Sorted everything out?'

'Yep.' Nate nodded.

Mike and I waited for him to elaborate, but he did not.

'Ah, I see. It is a secret?'

'*Sí.*' Carlos nodded.

'Fair enough,' said Mike.

I was intrigued to find out what Carlos had been keeping from Lily. She had not looked very happy since we had arrived, so I hoped that he would share it with her soon to allow her to enjoy Christmas Day tomorrow.

Once we got to the village, Nate asked where we should go first.

'Butcher's,' Mike suggested. 'I doubt they'll have a turkey, but it's worth a try.'

'Let's go,' Nate added.

Just as we were about to cross the street, the butcher came running out of his shop towards us. So did the lady from the supermarket.

Nate, Mike and Carlos looked at me and frowned.

'Quick!' the woman shouted. 'Emergency!' She stopped in front of us, trying to catch her breath. 'Your wife! She's having the baby!'

'*Merde!*' I shouted. My throat went dry and my pulse raced. 'How is she? And the baby?' I asked, quickly pulling my phone out, my heart thundering against my chest. 'Please tell me everything you know.'

'Rudy called us about forty-five minutes ago, but we told him you hadn't arrived yet. And then he called again fifteen minutes ago to say her waters had broken!'

'Fuck!' Nate's eyes widened. 'But are they okay?'

'I-I think so,' the supermarket lady replied. 'He said they're going to try calling the midwife. He's left his landline number so you can call him back.' She handed me a piece of paper.

I unlocked my phone, then dialled Miriam's number.

Cassie did not know, but Miriam had insisted that I call

her if the baby came early so that we could put the contingency plan I had prepared in place.

Even before we had arrived, I had been happy to agree not to use my connections—as long as it did not put Cassie or our child's safety at risk.

Nobody could question my commitment to honouring her wishes, but now things were different. This was an emergency, so I planned to use every resource available to me to keep them both safe.

'*Salut*,' Miriam answered.

'*Salut*. It is happening.'

'*Entendu*,' Miriam replied. 'I have the location. The midwife and the rest of the team will be on the helicopter in ten minutes. It should not take long for them to arrive at the cabin.'

'And the plough?'

'I am sending a message now. They will clear a path immediately. I will call someone to collect you from the village. *Ne t'inquiète pas*. Is there anything else?'

'Wi-Fi and everything that was on the list.'

'It will be done.'

Miriam ended the call.

My chest loosened. I was glad that the medical team would be on their way.

They were already in Scotland, staying in a nearby town. They had been since the day we had arrived. That was why the only hotels nearby that Bella and Nate had called were fully booked.

When Cassie had first suggested coming to this location for the Christmas holidays, I was not happy. I told her I preferred to stay in the city—somewhere close to the hospital. But this trip and location were something that she had dreamed of doing and I wanted to make her happy, so I had agreed.

Agreeing to come here was one thing. But staying in such a remote location just a few weeks before she was due to give birth without a contingency plan would be madness.

So I had hired the best midwife, obstetrician, gynaecologist, anaesthetist and paediatrician I could find.

I was aware that normally so many medical professionals would not be required to help deliver a baby. A midwife alone could be sufficient. But because of my past experience, I preferred to have extra expert hands nearby, just in case.

I had arranged for them all to stay at the hotel. I did not want to separate them from their families for too long during the holidays, so I had also paid for them to bring their loved ones, plus provided them with food and whatever they needed.

Oui—it was expensive, but I could not put a price on the health of my wife and our child. Especially when both of their lives were at stake.

I had thought about telling Cassie. But when she told me she was not happy with the amount of money that was being spent on this trip and insisted that we keep everything simple, I knew that if I told her what I had arranged, she would say it was not necessary. That I was worrying too much. So I kept it from her and decided that if we did not need medical assistance, I would tell Cassie once we were safely back in London. And if there was an emergency and we needed them, like we did now, I was sure she would be glad that I had intervened.

Sometimes what we think we want is not always what we need.

'What's going on?' Nate frowned. 'Was that your assistant?'

'*Oui*. The medical team will take a helicopter to the cabin now and a car will come to collect us shortly. I will explain more on the way.'

'Thank fuck for that!' Nate blew out a breath.

The first day we had walked to the town, although I had resisted calling my contacts for help with food and other materials, whilst the others were talking in the supermarket, I had stepped outside to send Miriam our location and a short voice note suggesting we should look into how we could get to and from the cabin if the weather continued to be bad. I had also listed some items I thought we would need. I wanted to be prepared.

'If you give me his number, I can call Rudy to let him know,' Carlos said. I handed him the piece of paper. 'He can give the message to the ladies. I am sure they will be relieved.'

'Good idea,' Nate added.

'Hope it all goes well,' the supermarket lady replied, and the butcher nodded in agreement before they both left.

'It's going to be fine.' Mike rested his hand on my shoulder to reassure me.

I swallowed the lump in my throat and my chest tightened.

When the lady from the shop had told me that Cassie was in labour, my immediate response was to make sure everything was organised. That she and our child would be taken care of as quickly as possible. But now, the reality hit me.

Cassie was in labour.

She was having our baby.

I was about to become a father.

This was not how I had imagined it to happen. Although I had anticipated that there was a possibility that the baby could come early, I had always thought I would be there with her. Holding her hand as our baby came into the world.

But even though Miriam was sending a 4x4 to collect us, the plough would still need to clear the snow so it was safe for us to drive, which would take time.

We had the helicopter, but that was for the doctors and the midwife. The priority was to get them to Cassie as quickly as possible. If they stopped to collect me, that delay could put Cassie and the baby in danger. I could not risk it.

The clock was ticking.

I had to find a way to get back to Cassie.

Fast.

I could not miss the birth of our first child.

20

CASSIE

'Owwwwch!' I screamed. 'I can't do this!'

The pain gripped me. It felt like my stomach was being squeezed into a tiny vice.

'Shit,' Bella said. 'That's five minutes. The contractions are getting more frequent. We need a midwife. This is happening a lot quicker than I thought.'

'Lily's still over at Rudy's, trying to get hold of her,' Melody replied. 'I'll get some water and some towels—just in case.'

I got up, stretched my arms out, then gripped the back of the sofa. I couldn't get comfortable. Bella stood beside me and rubbed my back. Paul joined her and did the same. I felt so bad that he had to see me like this.

'Do you want to take Paul to your room?' I panted, trying to breathe in and out deeply, hoping it would soothe the pain.

'Sweetheart, why don't you go and help Aunty Melody find some towels to help Aunty Cassie?' Paul nodded and ran out of the room. 'Mel or Lily can take him outside to play once we know the midwife's on her way. I need to stay here with you.'

'Even if we get through to her, the roads are still thick with snow. I'm not even sure if an ambulance could get up here to take me to the hospital.'

'I know you don't want to hear this, hon,' said Bella, 'but it might be time to use your connections. It sounds excessive, but could you maybe get a private jet or something? I know you can't fly, but the midwife can. And the rate your contractions are coming, there's no way she'll make it here before this baby arrives otherwise.'

'Yeah. I was just thinking that. I know private planes all add to the carbon footprint, but I don't see how else we're going to do this. Unless we can find a way to get Wi-Fi here, then maybe she could video call us with instructions on how you could deliver the baby?' I swallowed the lump in my throat, knowing it was a lot to ask.

'*Me?*' Bella's eyes practically flew from her sockets. 'I don't know if… I'm not qualified!'

'I know, I'm sorry. This is all my bloody fault! I still don't know if Nico and the guys are safe after trekking to the village. Now I'm in labour and he's going to miss the birth.' Tears streamed down my cheeks. 'I should've stayed in London instead of coming here. I shouldn't have had sex yesterday. I should've let Nico use his connections, I should've—'

'Sssh.' Bella rubbed my back again. '*Shoulda, woulda, coulda*—none of that will help you right now. We could try and find a local doctor or midwife and if that doesn't work, then of course, we'll all help deliver the baby. Don't worry. It's going to be fine.'

Melody and Paul returned with a bed sheet, which they

placed over the sofa, then they put a stack of towels on the coffee table.

'Come and sit down,' Melody said.

I slowly hobbled round to the other side of the sofa. Just as I sat back, Lily rushed into the room.

'The midwife is on her way. With a medical team. They'll be here in fifteen minutes. They just need to find a good place to land the helicopter.'

'Helicopter?' I frowned.

'Yep. Nico arranged it…'

'Nico?' I jumped in. 'You spoke to him? Is he okay?'

'Yeah, briefly. Everyone's okay.'

'Oh, thank God!' I breathed a sigh of relief. I never would've forgiven myself if something had happened to him or any of the guys.

'They're on their way back here. I don't know all the details of what was arranged, but it seems like it's under control. Anyway, the midwife wants to know if we can see the head…' Lily winced a little. 'I said I'd get back to her straight away.'

'Ouuucchhh! Fuuucck!' Another contraction ripped through me. 'I can't. This is too painful!' I screamed. 'Why and how do people do this?'

'It's gonna be okay, love.' Melody held my hand.

'Nico!' I cried out. 'I need Nico!'

I wasn't strong enough to get through this. I thought I would be, but I couldn't. Especially without Nico by my side.

'We need to… um…' Lily paused, her voice trembling. 'We have to find out if we can see the baby's head,' she repeated.

'Let's go and get some water, Paul.' Melody led him out of the room.

'Which one of you wants the pleasure of having a look at my vag?' I forced a smile, trying to add some humour to the situation, despite freaking out.

'I-I don't think I can.' Lily gripped the arm of the sofa.

'Maybe we can do it together,' Bella suggested. 'Cass, we're going to need you to lie back and open your legs wide so we can take a look. Okay?'

I nodded. I couldn't talk anymore.

As I lifted my bum up from the sofa, they slid down my giant granny pants and peered between my legs. Just as I looked up to gauge their reaction, Lily's eyes rolled back and she collapsed on the floor.

'Shit!' I shouted, just as another intense contraction hit me, causing me to let out a strangled cry.

'Lily!' Bella turned to see her crumpled on the floor. 'Lily!' she repeated, laying her down on her back and kneeling beside her.

'What's going on?' Melody ran into the room. 'Fuck! What happened?'

'We were trying to see if we could see the baby's head and Lily passed out,' Bella said.

'Is… is Lily okay?' I asked, desperately trying to calm myself down and breathe through the contraction. 'Could you see the head?'

'Lily should be fine in a minute. Don't freak out, but I can definitely see the head. This baby is coming!' Bella mopped her damp forehead with the back of her hand. She was normally the calm one, but I could tell that even she was shitting bricks.

'She's still breathing.' Melody knelt down beside Lily

and gently rested her hand on Lily's chest. 'She's probably not been that close to another woman's fanny before and she got overwhelmed!' Melody cackled. Bella glared. 'Sorry, wrong time to joke. Paul's playing in the other room, so tell me what I can do to help.'

'Try and see if you can get Lily to wake up, whilst I attempt to help Cassie give birth to this baby. I don't think it wants to wait until the midwife arrives…'

'No probs! A gentle slap around the chops or splashing some water on her face should do the trick!'

'No! Don't do any of that! Just raise her legs and…'

'Hold on, she's opening her eyes!' Melody said.

Just as Lily regained consciousness, we heard voices in the hallway and then a group of strangers burst into the room.

'You must be Cassie,' the shorter woman said as she quickly removed her coat. 'I'm Clara: your midwife. This is Dr Blitzen, your obstetrician, Dr Khan, your gynaecologist, Dr Dasher, your anaesthetist, and Dr Fisayo, your paediatrician. We're here to deliver your baby and take care of you.'

'Oh thank God!' Bella exhaled loudly.

I was also relieved to know that the cavalry had arrived.

But Nico wasn't here.

I knew how much he was looking forward to being there to support me.

I knew how much he wanted to see our child brought into the world. And now he was going to miss the birth.

Because of me.

I didn't know how I'd ever be able to forgive myself.

21

NICO

We were on our way.

The plough had cleared a path, and the driver of the extra-large 4x4 that had collected us said it should not take too much longer to get to the cabin.

I had considered calling the helicopter back to get us, but I needed that to be on standby for Cassie. Just in case…

I swallowed hard, hoping that it would not be required, but Miriam had already spoken with the nearest hospital and alerted the staff.

The driver had brought a device which would allow us to use Wi-Fi.

I tried calling Rudy again.

No answer.

Sweat trickled down my forehead. I was trying to stay calm, but it was difficult. I needed to see my wife. To hold her hand. To wipe her brow and tell her that everything was going to be okay. Even if right now I was not sure that it would be.

'You okay, bro?' Nate rested his hand on my shoulder.

I shook my head. My heart and mind were racing so quickly I was worried I would pass out. I inhaled deeply, then exhaled. It was important to stay strong. I could not let Cassie or our baby down.

'This is my fault. I should have listened to my instincts. I knew that coming somewhere so remote was not a good idea.'

'C'mon, man. Don't beat yourself up about this. You and I both know that when my sister gets her heart set on something, nothing will change her mind. And anyway, there was no way of knowing the baby would decide to come early.'

'It is my fault.' I hung my head and my eyes watered as guilt flooded my chest.

'Why d'you say that?'

'I… we…' It was difficult trying to say this to Nate, but he needed to know I was responsible. 'Yesterday, Cassie and I… we made love. I was worried that it would make the baby come early and I was right.'

I exhaled again, preparing myself for Nate's anger. I deserved it.

'Listen.' His voice softened. 'I don't know much about childbirth and labour, but I'm pretty sure that's a myth.'

'Nate's right,' Mike added. 'You're not to blame. One of my friends' baby didn't come on the due date. They tried everything, having sex multiple times, baths, exercise —all the things you hear about and still nothing. In the end, his wife had to be induced. Bella and I had sex during the last couple of weeks before Paul came and it made no difference. At the end of the day, if a woman's body isn't ready to give birth, nothing will make it happen. Cassie was probably ready to go into labour and it would've happened today with or without you getting it on.'

Hearing that made me feel a little better, but the only thing that would ease the sharp pain in my chest was being there with her.

'I think we are here,' Carlos said.

As I saw the cabin in sight, my head bolted upright. The driver slowed down and I undid my seat belt, without waiting for him to turn off the engine. Before he had pulled over, I jumped out of the 4x4, ran to the front door, then raced inside, heading straight to the living room.

Cassie was lying on the sofa, crying out with the medical team around her as the midwife stood between Cassie's legs, telling her to push.

'Nico!' she sobbed and my heart broke. 'I need my husband!'

I ran to her.

'I am here, *chérie*.' I grabbed her hand and kissed her forehead.

'You're… you're here!' Tears streamed down her cheeks. 'I thought you weren't…. *owwww!*'

'It is okay,' I said softly. Bella handed me a damp flannel and I wiped the sweat from Cassie's forehead. 'Everything will be okay.' She gripped my hand tightly. 'You are doing so well.'

Cassie continued to follow the instructions from the medical team, pushing when she was told. I kept squeezing her hand and encouraging her as much as I could, whilst I tried to keep my own emotions under control.

I was relieved I was here. I would not have wanted her to go through this alone. Even though her best friends were here to support her, I knew it was not the same.

Cassie gave one more big push, and seconds later the sound of our baby's high-pitched cries filled the room.

'Congratulations!' The midwife beamed. 'You have a beautiful baby girl!'

I looked at the tiny baby in her arms and froze.

We had a little girl.

We were parents.

After cutting the cord, the midwife wrapped our baby in a blanket and handed her to Cassie, who burst into tears.

As I stared at our child, I went to speak but the words would not come. This was… unreal.

'Thank you.' I looked at Cassie, then back at our daughter, swallowing the lump in my throat.

I could not believe what I had just witnessed.

Our precious daughter had arrived. On Christmas Eve.

Cassie had just given birth to our child and I was completely in awe.

'She's beautiful,' Cassie gushed, resting our baby on her chest. 'Even with all my gunk and blood over her,' she laughed. 'Hello, little one. I'm your mummy. Would you like to meet your daddy?'

Cassie handed her to me and my eyes widened. Even though I had had many months to prepare for this, I was still nervous.

I can do this.

As I took our daughter in my arms and my eyes met hers, the emotions became too much. Warm tears rolled down my cheeks.

I had enjoyed many special moments in my life. Meeting Cassie, then marrying the love of my life. But *this* —this moment here, becoming a father—was the most amazing of them all.

22

CASSIE

'The car is outside.' Nico held my coat up behind me. I slid my arms into the sleeves.

We were at the hospital. Although the medical team had checked me and our daughter over thoroughly yesterday before they'd left, they'd recommended that we both come by just to be sure.

Luckily we'd been given the thumbs up, so now we were ready to go back to the cabin.

'One moment.' Nico glanced down at his phone. 'Wait here.' He walked out of the private room to take a call. He'd taken a few calls already this morning. Probably more people congratulating him or wishing him a merry Christmas.

I looked down at the car seat that was resting on the bed, holding our baby.

Our *baby*.

I was a mum. I still couldn't believe it.

When our little girl had woken up crying this morning, it took a while to register where the noise was coming from. And then I remembered. Crazy to think that twenty-four hours ago she was cocooned in my stomach and now she was here. Out in the big wide world.

She'd been sleeping for the past half an hour and I couldn't take my eyes off her.

Although they were closed now, she had huge dark brown eyes, along with thick jet-black curly hair and chubby cheeks that you just wanted to shower with kisses. I was so in love.

I'd spoken to Mum and Dad briefly yesterday after Nate had used the Wi-Fi thing Nico had organised, to let them know they were now officially grandparents. I was surprised my hearing was still intact after how loud they'd screamed down the phone.

After their initial elation, Mum had said how lucky I was that it had turned out okay. She was right. Thank God Nico had had that plan in place. He'd told me everything earlier and I was so grateful.

'Come.' Nico returned to the room and picked up the car seat. 'Let us go.'

I must've fallen asleep because when I opened my eyes after hearing Nico call my name, we were pulling up in front of the cabin.

OMG.

As Nico helped me out of the car, my mouth fell open.

The cabin had been decorated with beautiful fairy lights. There were twelve gold glitter reindeers with a red glitter Santa sleigh, complete with a replica of the man himself dressed in his red-and-white suit, clutching a sack of presents resting on the snow at the front of the cabin.

Although the roads were much clearer now and the snow had stopped, there was still a beautiful sheet of snow covering the ground. I'd got the white Christmas I'd hoped for.

'You… when did you…?' I was speechless.

'Whilst we were at the hospital a team came to set it up.'

'I love it!' I gushed.

Nico smiled as he took the seat from the car. As we arrived at the cabin's entrance, a gorgeous scent flooded my nostrils. A beautiful festive wreath, made with pine cones, dried orange and lemon slices, cinnamon sticks, colourful berries and a huge red ribbon hung on the front door.

As I stepped inside the warm cabin, my mouth fell open again as I took in the beautiful curtain of fairy lights which lined the walls and the festive garlands that adorned the picture frames.

Ariana Grande's 'Santa Tell Me' played softly through the little black speakers that were on the floor. My heart fluttered as I remembered that song playing when Nico and I spent our first Christmas Day together as we cooked lunch in my tiny kitchen.

'Is that you, Cass?' I heard Melody call out from the living room. I looked behind me to see if our little one had woken up, but she still seemed fast asleep.

'Yeah,' I said quietly.

'Can you help me with something in here, please, love?'

'Course!' I stepped inside and—

Holy shit.

'Surprise!'

I almost fainted as I took in my surroundings. It wasn't just that the room had been decorated with festive red stockings hanging from the fireplace, but also the fact that the room was filled with people.

And not just any people. All of my nearest and dearest.

Mum and Dad were here, along with Sophia, Lorenzo and Leo, my eldest sister, Flo, and her husband, Darren. They were all dressed in an assortment of cheesy red Christmas jumpers, which brought an even bigger smile to my face.

'You're… I can't believe you're all here!' Happy tears streamed down my cheeks.

Mum and Dad rushed over and pulled me into a hug.

'Congrats, sweetheart! Oh, and Merry Christmas!' Dad said. 'Bet you won't forget this Christmas in a hurry!'

'Nope!' I laughed.

I caught sight of the Christmas tree that Nico and the boys had brought to the cabin yesterday. I loved that it hadn't been replaced with a new, fancy tree or decorations. Knowing that the tree was dressed with a combination of vintage decorations that'd been used by Rudy and his family for years and the ones we'd made by hand yesterday was perfect.

'Can we see her?' Mum looked over at Nico, who was by the door, smiling and cradling our little girl in his arms. She was awake now, her big brown eyes wide open. My heart swelled with joy.

'Of course!' he brought her closer.

'Oh my goodness! She is perfect!' Mum gushed as a crowd gathered round us.

'I'm so happy for you both,' Flo added. 'She's gorgeous.'

'She really is!' said Lily. 'Sorry again for fainting on

you yesterday. I think I just got a bit overwhelmed with it all and seeing the head and…'

'No worries!' I said.

'She's got your eyes, love,' Dad cooed. 'Have you decided what to call her yet?'

I looked at Nico and he wrapped his arm around my waist.

'We have. We'll tell you all at lunch. Speaking of which…' My nostrils twitched. 'Is that turkey I can smell?'

'*Oui.*' Nico smiled again. 'Lunch will be ready soon.'

After I'd finished giving everyone hugs and kisses and they'd cooed over our little bundle of joy, we all headed over to the dining table and I gasped as I took in the elegant festive display.

The table was dressed with shiny gold cutlery and plates, crystal glasses and thick red cloth napkins.

An extra table and set of chairs had been added to the main oak table so that everyone could fit. It all looked amazing.

The chef came into the dining room to introduce herself and asked if I was ready for lunch to be served. After checking with everyone, I gave her the green light.

'Room for one more?' I heard Rudy's voice boom. When I looked up, my mouth fell open. He was dressed in a Santa outfit that looked *very* authentic.

'Of course!' I replied.

'We wondered where you'd got to!' Melody said, pulling out a chair. 'We didn't see you last night and when Lily and I came to find you earlier there was no answer.'

'I was busy last night and this morning...' Rudy smiled.

'Busy doing what, eh? Delivering presents?' Melody raised her eyebrow.

'Now that would be telling...'

'Santa!' Paul ran into the room with Leo beside him. 'Mum! Dad! Santa is here for lunch!'

'Great, son!' Mike patted him on the head as they all sat down.

Everyone quickly filed in around the table, took their seats and wasted no time getting stuck into the delicious feast of roast turkey, crisp roast potatoes, Brussels sprouts, pigs in blankets, stuffing, parsnips, nut roast and an assortment of other treats.

As I listened to the rumble of laughter, mixed with the gentle sound of Mariah Carey's 'All I Want for Christmas' playing in the background and the *mmms* and *ahhhs* of satisfaction that vibrated around the room, I smiled. Everything was perfect. But it could've all been so different. And I wasn't just talking about the birth of our child.

Right now, if Nico hadn't intervened, we might've been eating soup for Christmas lunch instead of this delicious turkey.

Instead of spending time chatting together, we would've all been rushed off our feet trying to get everything prepared. There was nothing wrong with that, of course. It's what probably ninety-nine per cent of the population did. It was all I'd ever known growing up. But that didn't mean it was the only way to celebrate Christmas.

Nico and I were so lucky to have the opportunity to make things extra special for our family. To give them a chance to relax and put their feet up and take time off from cooking. So why shouldn't we give them that?

I'd got it wrong. I'd thought that lavishing them with treats would make them think I was showing off, and I'd nearly ruined our holiday because of it.

'I'd like to say a few words.' I stood up, tapping my fork on the side of my glass. The table fell silent. 'I'd like to apologise.'

'For what?' Melody frowned.

'For not giving you all the luxury holiday you were expecting. Although the fire at the cabin and the heavy snow were out of our control, we might have been able to get better supplies here a bit earlier if we'd used Nico's contacts. But that would've meant getting a plane or helicopter or hiring special equipment to clear the roads and I didn't want you to think that we were being OTT. As you ladies know, that's why we didn't go ahead with hiring a full-time chef, entertainers and other stuff. But the thing is, Nico's kind of rich.'

'I'll say!' Dad laughed.

'And seeing as we're married and have a baby together now, I guess that means I am too. So I'm going to try and embrace it a bit more! Don't worry, that doesn't mean going full-on la-di-da—'

'Good!' Mum jumped in.

'It just means that sometimes we're going to spend and enjoy that money. And hopefully you'll be there to enjoy it with us too.'

'*Oh, the hardship!*' Lily laughed.

'But of course, if ever you think I've become a stuck-up cow or am getting too big for my boots, let me know so I can nip it in the bud, pronto!'

'Don't worry,' said Nate. 'We will!'

'Great!' The baby cried and I got up and picked her up from her basket. 'So now that this little one is awake, maybe it's time to let you know the name we've chosen for her.'

The whole table cooed with excitement.

'We are going to call her Nicola,' Nico said.

'I love my husband's name and I'd love the idea of her having something similar. Plus, seeing as she was born so close to Christmas, it kind of felt fitting and it ties in with the whole French Saint Nicolas thing too, so…'

'I love it!' said Sophia.

'It's wonderful,' Mum added, and everyone agreed.

Nicola decided that was the perfect moment to scream down the cabin.

'Looks like someone needs feeding! I'll be back soon, but in the meantime, please enjoy the rest of your lunch!'

I headed to the bedroom and Nico followed. I could've tried feeding her at the table, but I wanted everyone to enjoy eating in peace.

After lifting up my top and pulling out my boob, I put Nicola on my breast. This was going to take some getting used to.

'Everything okay, *chérie*?'

'Yeah, all good! You don't have to stay, you can go back and make sure everyone's okay.'

Nico's phone chimed. After days without our phones and the internet, it would take a while to get used to hearing phone notification pings again.

He glanced at the screen.

'It is Carlos. He has asked if he could speak to us when we have a moment.'

'Sounds serious. I don't think things are a hundred per cent with him and Lily yet, so let him know it's okay to come now.' I draped a cloth over my shoulder to cover my breast.

'Okay, I will bring him here.'

A few minutes later Carlos entered the room. He sat down on the chair and explained why he'd been acting weird. It all made sense now.

Once Nicola finished her feed, Nico burped her, then hushed her to sleep before we all returned to the table.

As Lily's gaze followed Carlos, I knew that like everyone else she wanted to find out what had been happening.

And based on what Carlos had just told us, she wouldn't have to wait long to find out…

23

———

CASSIE

'I would like to say a few words.' Carlos stood up from the table. Lily's eyes widened. 'Some of you may have noticed that I have been a little… *distracted* since we have been at the cabin. I have had some things on my mind and now I am ready to share them with you, particularly with the very special lady in my life.'

Carlos walked around to the other side of the table, where Lily was sitting. As Carlos reached into his pocket and dropped down onto one knee, Lily frowned, then gasped.

'Oh my God!' she said and the whole table grinned as the realisation of what was happening hit them.

'Lily, you are the most precious person in the world to me and I want to spend the rest of my life with you. I wanted to make this proposal special, so I had a ring designed for you. That is why I was hiding my phone, so you would not see the many messages from the designer, and that is where I went on those Saturdays and said you could not come with me. I wanted it to be a surprise. And I had big plans to propose the day before we came here, but everything went wrong. I wanted to do something big—bigger than when I surprised you that night we officially got together.'

'It wouldn't have mattered.' Lily's voice cracked. She already had tears in her eyes.

'I just wanted things to be perfect. I was disappointed because I wanted you to have the ring for Christmas. So we could celebrate the good news with our friends and family. I told myself that when we arrived at the cabin, I could organise something else, but then… well, there was no phone reception or internet and our options were limited, so I became more frustrated with myself. I had to keep it a secret, because I know that with a proposal, it is best when it is a surprise and many women like it to be memorable. Special. I did not want to let you down.'

'Oh, I wouldn't have thought that!'

'And then when you started to ignore me, I was concerned that maybe you were having second thoughts about us and… I was worried about proposing and you saying no. But then when Nate was angry and you spoke to me, I realised you thought my secrecy meant that I did not want you. Everything became a mess and it is my fault. I should have handled it differently. I am sorry.'

'It's okay.' Lily stroked his cheek.

'I did not know what to do. I thought about waiting until we got back to plan something else big and romantic for New Year's Eve instead, but I did not want to wait anymore. Then someone wise told me that you would not mind if I did not do something grand'—he looked over at Nate—'so, here I am. In front of more people than I had planned. Asking you, Quesito, the love of my life, if you would like to become my wife.'

As Carlos opened the box, tears ran down Lily's cheeks.

The whole room held their breath, eagerly awaiting her response.

'Come on, Lil,' Nate called out. 'Put the poor guy out of his misery!' he laughed.

'Yes!' She grinned. 'A million times, yes!'

Carlos let out a sigh of relief before sliding the diamond ring down Lily's finger. She jumped up and they threw their arms around one another before kissing passionately on the lips.

'Kids, cover your eyes!' Melody cackled.

Carlos pulled away slowly and held Lily's gaze.

'And there is another reason why I have been acting a little distracted and been worried about talking…'

Oh… I didn't know he had something else to tell her. My mind raced, wondering what it could be.

'It's okay.' Lily stroked his cheek. 'You can tell me anything. Unless you want to do it privately?' She glanced around the table and saw everyone's eyes fixated on them. I knew they were itching to pass on their congratulations, but now Carlos had declared he had more news, they were all holding their breaths.

'In some ways it involves your family, so it is okay.' He paused. 'I have been offered a six-month residency. But it is in Australia and I was worried about leaving my best friend for that long and taking you away from your family. Cassie is already in Paris, but it is easy to travel there and I did not want to—'

'Let's do it!' Lily jumped in. 'A couple of years ago,

the thought of travelling halfway across the world would've scared the shit out of me, but since we got together in Spain, I love going to different places. And you never know, maybe the club will want to hire me to as one of their professional dancers!'

The table fell silent.

'I know your dance skills have improved massively, Lil,' Nate jumped in, 'but I'm not sure you're quite at pro level… *yet*.' He smiled.

'I'm joking!' Everyone breathed a sigh of relief. 'I've got enough of my own clients, and as long as I have my laptop and internet access, I can do their accounts from anywhere in the world. And I reckon Australia will be amazing!'

'*Genial!*' Carlos's face brightened. 'I thought you would think it was too far—especially with your new niece.'

'We can video call. And it's only six months. What's half a year when we have the rest of our lives to spend together? And as for little Nicola, babies just sleep, eat and poo a lot for the first few months, don't they?'

'You're not wrong!' Melody laughed.

'Exactly! So we'll be back before she starts doing all the really fun stuff like crawling, walking and talking. It'll be fine!'

Carlos threw his arms around Lily again and the whole table cheered before getting up, then rushing over to congratulate them.

There were lots of hugs, kisses and happy tears. It was so lovely to see Lily smiling again.

'Told you he wasn't playing away,' Melody said as she gave Lily another squeeze.

'Damn right,' Nate said. 'Best friend or not, he knew I'd cut his dick off.'

'Nathaniel!' Mum shouted. 'Language!'

'Chill, Mum. I'm joking! The poor guy has been tying himself up in knots, worrying about leaving his best mate for six months.' He shook his head. 'I mean, I know being apart from me will be traumatic for him,' he laughed, 'but I'm a big man, I can handle not having Carlitos around for a while. Like I said during our talk, the main thing is that you're both happy.' Nate patted Carlos on the back.

'I'll take care of him,' Melody added. 'And I'm not offended that you didn't ask me to create Lily's engagement ring…' She raised her eyebrow.

'I considered it,' Carlos replied, 'but I wanted the proposal to be a surprise, and no offence, but I know how you ladies like to talk… I did not even tell Nate until yesterday.'

'I'd like to say I would've kept it a secret, but, yeah, I probably would've been too excited to keep my gob shut!' Melody laughed.

'But I'd love you to do my wedding ring, if you'd like?' Lily said.

'Course!'

I was glad that everything had worked out.

Earlier Carlos had come to ask me and Nico if we minded him proposing to Lily here and now. He was conscious that today was a day for celebrating Nicola's birth and didn't want to gatecrash. We assured him that we didn't mind at all. There was no such thing as too much good news, and we wanted him and Lily to be happy.

'Congratulations!' Lorenzo lifted his champagne flute in the air to toast the happy couple.

'To Lily and Carlos!' Sophia clinked her glass against his and everyone joined in.

'Such wonderful news!' Mum beamed. 'Finally, all of my children are settled. Flo and Darren, Cassie and Nico and now Lily and Carlos.'

'Well, Lily and Carlos were settled before he proposed, love,' Dad added.

'Yes, I know, but now it's *official*. And I never thought I'd see the day, but even Nate has settled down. Maybe one day he'll put a ring on Melody's finger too…' The corner of her mouth twitched.

As much as Mum had always liked Melody, it had taken a while for her to get used to Nate and Melody being together, especially after what had happened with them at our wedding reception. But now, she was happy that they'd found love together.

'Yeah, you never know.' Nate grinned and the whole table's mouths fell to the floor.

Even though we knew Nate was head over heels, we'd all expected him to laugh it off or say something funny, but nope. Melody clearly was the one.

'I like the sound of that,' Melody smiled.

'I know I've been hogging the mic, so to speak, a lot today,' I said, 'but Mum's words have made me think of something. Exactly two years ago today, I was at my old flat in London, spending Christmas with a Frenchman I'd only met forty-eight hours before. Little did I know that if we fast-forwarded to this day we'd be here, married, with a beautiful daughter, celebrating with you all. And I never would've thought that Lily would be with Nate's bestie, Carlos, and definitely not that Nate would be with Melody!'

'That makes two of us!' Melody threw her head back laughing.

'But yet, here we are. All loved up, all happy, all living our best lives. I used to think Christmas was cursed, but now, despite the little setback of our cabin being on fire, I see that some of the happiest times in my life have happened at this time of year. Right now, I feel like my life is perfect. This is my perfect happy ending. The road ahead won't always be smooth, but with each other, we'll still find a way to smile and be happy.'

'Hear, hear!' Bella said.

'So I'd like to raise another toast: to each and every one of us. To Mum and Dad, to our kind host, Rudy, Paul, Leo, our precious Nicola and to our couples: Sophia and Lorenzo, Mike and Bella, Melody and Nate, me and Nico, and of course to our newly engaged lovebirds, Lily and Carlos. It was a struggle for many of us to find *the one*, but we've all got our happily-ever-afters! Here's to many more happy years and celebrations to come!'

After everyone had hugged and finished Christmas lunch, we all leant back, feeling like a bunch of stuffed turkeys.

'Aunty Cassie, is it time to open the presents now?' Paul asked loudly. 'Santa said he'd left some for me and Leo under the tree.'

Oh yeah. I'd been so overwhelmed by seeing all the decorations and everyone in the living room, I hadn't noticed that there were presents under the tree too.

I looked up at Rudy and he winked. Was he responsible for the gifts or had Nico arranged for new presents to be delivered because the ones I'd ordered had been destroyed in the fire?

'Of course!' I replied.

As we all walked towards the tree, something dawned on me. I turned to Nico, who had a sleepy Nicola cradled in his arms.

'I haven't got you a gift!'

'You would like to give me something?' he asked.

'Course!'

'I know what I would like…' He took my hand, led me outside the living room and pointed above the door frame. I looked up and saw sprigs of mistletoe hanging from it. I hadn't noticed that before.

'You don't need mistletoe to get a kiss from me!' I stood on tiptoe, leant forward, being careful not to crush our little one, and pressed my lips against his. My whole body trembled and a warm feeling filled my stomach, like a mug of hot chocolate.

'Just like on the rooftop bar, that first night we met,' Nico said softly.

'Yep! Just in case you didn't know, you already have a lifetime supply of kisses from me. If you want, I can write it on a piece of paper and make it into a gift voucher, so it'll be like a proper present. Well, sort of!' I laughed.

'*Chérie*.' Nico slipped his arm around my waist and looked into my eyes, then at Nicola and back at me again, before pressing another tender kiss on my lips. 'You have already given me more presents than I can count. When you came to live with me in Paris, you gave me your heart. When you agreed to marry me, you gave me the most amazing wife a man could ask for. And now you have given me a child. *A family*. My life is complete. I do not need anything more. With you and Nicola, I have the greatest gifts of all.'

One Year Later

As I approached the solid oak dining table and took in the sight of the festive display in front of me, my heart skipped a beat. This time one year ago, Nico and I were celebrating Christmas and the birth of our daughter with our close friends and family. And now here we were, back at the place where everything happened, celebrating Nicola's first birthday.

The sounds of laughter echoed in the air. Nicola let out a little chuckle.

'What are you laughing about, little one?' I pecked her gently on her head, wrapping my arms tighter around her. I couldn't believe how much she'd grown. Time was going too quickly for my liking.

'Ma-ma.' Nicola looked at me with her beautiful big

brown eyes and smiled, causing my stomach to flip. I'd never tire of hearing her say that. 'Da-da.'

'You want to go to Daddy?' I asked, handing her over to Nico.

Every day she looked more and more like him. She had his long lashes, his nose, and even though she only had half a dozen teeth, with any luck, she'd end up having his dazzling smile too.

She didn't get all of her features from him, though. Her dark, thick curly hair definitely came from me.

'I was about to send out a search party!' Mum said as I sat down at the table.

'It took a while to clean up her nappy explosion!' I laughed. I still didn't understand how something so cute and little could do such a big poo, but hey, it was what babies did.

Alma, the nanny, had offered to change her, but I said I'd do it. Few things were more humbling than changing your little girl's dirty nappy.

Yep, that's right. We had a nanny. I knew having a baby would be hard work, but the reality was even more challenging than I'd thought. Especially in the early days when little Nicky was demanding to be fed every two hours. I had the opportunity to get help, so there was no shame in asking for it. I'd just be cutting off my nose to spite my face. So after interviewing dozens of candidates, we'd finally chosen Alma, who'd been brilliant.

I was so surprised when Mum came to visit us a week after Alma had started. I expected that she'd scoff about us hiring help, but she said that she thought it was a great idea.

'If I had the opportunity to have a nanny, the help and

all the things you have, I would've grabbed it with both hands!' she'd said. 'I'm sorry if I was too hard on you before. Just because things were difficult for me and your father back in the day, it doesn't mean you should go through that too. And just because we didn't have money when we were raising you doesn't mean you're selling out if you do. You and Nico earn your money fair and square. It'd be criminal not to make the most of the opportunities you have. Enjoy it, girl!'

And she was right. There was nothing wrong for asking for help or enjoying a bit of luxury. You could still be loaded and be a good person.

These days I felt less guilty about spending money. Don't get me wrong, I wasn't frivolous. I didn't go into restaurants and throw money in the air or order the most expensive dishes on the menu. I just didn't feel so bad about shelling out for things that made me or our loved ones happy.

For example, I knew that Flo and Darren had been struggling to conceive for years, so we'd paid for them to see the best doctors and start IVF treatment.

It'd taken multiple rounds, but now Flo was three months pregnant and over the moon. Of course my parents were beside themselves with excitement when they heard they'd be getting a second grandchild.

That alone proved that money could definitely be used for good.

When I was organising the Christmas celebrations, this time I didn't feel guilty about spoiling our guests. Especially Rudy.

Without his kindness last Christmas, things wouldn't have been the same. That's why this year we'd paid for

Rudy's family to travel first class from Australia to Scotland so that we could all celebrate together.

We were just strangers and yet he'd opened up his home and his heart to help us out when we were in need. And that would never be forgotten.

This was the second time Rudy had seen his family this year. Nico and I hated the fact that he hadn't seen his daughter for over a decade and had never met his grandson in person. Seeing how much Mum and Dad adored Nicky, I could never imagine how difficult it would be for them to be kept apart for so long.

That's why, once we got back to London after Boxing Day, we contacted Rudy and offered to cover the cost of flying his daughter, her husband and their son over to visit. Seeing photos of their happy reunion together was priceless.

We'd also covered the costs of refurbishing the cabin. The floorboards and electrics had been fixed, there was a new kitchen and bathroom (including a sturdy sink) and of course we'd replaced the beds…

A smaller cabin had also been built on the land at our expense, with a few extra bedrooms so there'd be room for our family and friends to stay when they visited, which was something we planned to do often. Perhaps it would become an annual Christmas tradition?

The cabin had still kept all of its charm and was now a B&B just like Rudy's wife had always wanted.

It looked so gorgeous that even the dickhead owner of the posh cabin we were originally supposed to stay at offered to buy it from Rudy.

After the fire (which was apparently caused by someone leaving a lit cigarette in the cabin after moving our stuff inside), the pompous twat wanted to expand his resort to make more money.

Thankfully, Rudy told him to stick his offer where the sun didn't shine because the cabin wasn't for sale.

On the subject of the cabin, or more specifically, the couple who'd demolished its original sink, Melody and Nate were both doing really well. Melody had left her job and was now running Flame Designs full-time. I'd lost count of how many countries her jewellery was being sold in and the celebs that were wearing her stuff on the red carpet.

Speaking of celebs, ever since he'd trained a big Hollywood actor earlier this year, Nate's personal training business had blown up. He was successful before, but the amount he charged for sessions now was eyewatering. He deserved every penny, though.

They were both doing well professionally, but there'd been an amazing development with their personal life too…

Nate had recently proposed and of course Mel had said yes. So next year we had *two* weddings to attend: Melody and Nate's and Lily and Carlos's.

Lily and Carlos were also doing great. They'd had an amazing time in Australia. Rudy had put them in touch with his daughter, who they'd met up with a few times, which was lovely.

Bella and Mike were stronger than ever. Work had picked up again for Bella, so they were fine financially. They were even speaking about taking time away from London and travelling around Asia with Paul.

After they'd lived in Vietnam for a couple of years when they'd first got together, that part of the world held a special place in their hearts, and they reckoned it would easier to show Paul where his parents had lived whilst he was young rather than when he started secondary school in a few years.

Sophia, Lorenzo and Leo were also doing great. Apparently, Lorenzo had been offered an incredible opportunity that could change their fortunes.

We tried to get Sophia to spill the beans, but they'd signed an NDA which said it needed to be kept secret for the moment. But she promised to share news with us as soon as she was able to.

As Nico tickled Nicky's stomach, she laughed and it was the sweetest sound.

I always knew Nico would be an amazing father, but he'd surpassed my expectations. The way he looked at our daughter like she was the most perfect human ever created never failed to make my heart swell. He'd do anything for Nicky. He'd do anything for both of us. It was crazy to think she'd only been in our lives for such a short space of time but had quickly become the centre of our universe.

Things between me and Nico were great. With his therapist, he'd worked through the trauma of his past and was able to speak about it more openly. We'd also added a pregnancy and baby loss charity to the list of groups we supported.

If that contribution could give just one person the help they needed so that they didn't suffer for years like Nico had, it'd be worth it.

Our business and charitable ventures were thriving, I was working part-time from home so I had more time to spend with our daughter, and we were adjusting well to being a family of three.

Life was more hectic, but Nico and I still tried to enjoy our time as a couple, including finding time to have fun in the bedroom. Yep… things were definitely back on track in that department.

'Awww,' Doris cooed as she came to stand beside Nico and touched Nicky's hand. 'I'm so glad I survived long enough to meet your little one and to see Lily planning her wedding. I'd rather hoped that *I* would've found hubby number eight by now.'

As always, Doris, our eighty-nine-year-old friend, looked glam with her smoky eyes, red lips and chic silver hair which matched her silky dress.

'Don't give up hope!' Lily laughed. 'A lot can change in a year. Just ask Mel and Nate.'

'Too bloody right!' Melody cackled, flashing her sparkly red-and-gold ring in the air.

Melody hadn't gone the conventional route for her engagement ring. She'd designed it herself. To be expected from London's hottest jewellery designer.

'Many congratulations to you too. Although, technically, I should be jealous because in Provence, Nathaniel, your now fiancé, had promised to keep *me* in mind to be his bride and then you jumped in and snapped him up. But no hard feelings.'

The whole table erupted into a fit of laughter. Oh how we loved Doris.

'Maybe you'd like to join me for a drink later.' Rudy smiled at Doris, his eyes twinkling.

'That sounds wonderful.' Doris smiled. 'If you don't mind me asking, how old are you, dear?'

'Eighty-one years young,' Rudy replied without hesitation.

'Excellent!' Doris clapped her hands together. 'I've always loved a toy boy!'

As the table burst into a fit of giggles again, my heart filled with joy.

I looked around me. Nico was bouncing Nicky on his knee, Lily and Carlos were gazing into each other's eyes, Nate was stroking Melody's cheek and Mike, Bella and Paul were laughing together and everyone was deep in conversation. Everything couldn't be more perfect.

'What are you thinking about, *chérie*?'

'Just about how far we've come.'

'*Oui.* A lot has changed since we first met, Mademoiselle Fraise.' The corner of his mouth twitched, and I laughed as I remembered the nickname he'd first given me.

'It has, *dickhead*! Oops!' I quickly glanced at Nicky. The last thing I wanted was for her to learn that word and start using it. Luckily, she was too busy playing with her cuddly toy.

'I cannot believe you used to call me this!' Nico pretended to gasp.

'I know!' I chuckled. 'I'm glad I was wrong about you. You're definitely *not* a dickhead. You're amazing and you make me so happy! For so long, I thought that this kind of joy only happened in books and fairy tales. I still can't believe all this is real.'

'But it is. You are my queen and *ma petite chérie* is our princess. *This* is my fairy tale. The two of you are everything that I have ever wanted.'

'Same. I said it last year and I meant it. This is my perfect happy ending.'

'*Oui.* Although this is just the beginning of our story.'

'If this is the beginning, what do you think will happen next?'

'That is obvious.'

'What are you? A clairvoyant?' I laughed.

'*Non.* I do not need a crystal ball. I can already tell you what will happen next in just six words.'

'Go on, then.' I smiled as my eyes met his.

'*We will live happily ever after.*'

I liked the sound of that.

Nico pecked Nicky on the head, causing her to squeal with joy.

And as Nico leant forward to kiss me softly on the lips, in that moment I knew that his prediction of our happy future together was destined to come true.

Not ready to say goodbye to the characters? Get FREE **bonus content here:** https://bookhip.com/GMCWKXQ

Have you read all of the other books in the series?

Book 1: *My Ten-Year Crush* (Bella and Mike)
Book 2: *My Lucky Night* (Cassie and Nico)
Book 3: *My Paris Romance* (Cassie and Nico)
Book 4: *My Spanish Romance* (Lily and Carlos)
Book 5: *My French Wedding Date* (Melody and Nate)
You can also read about Sophia and Lorenzo's story in *The Middle-Aged Virgin* series.

If you enjoyed this book, you'll love my new steamy fake-dating romcom, *The Match Faker*.
All books available to order from Amazon.

The Middle-Aged Virgin Series
The Middle-Aged Virgin
The Middle-Aged Virgin in Italy

Only When it's Love Series
Only When It's Love
When's the Wedding?

My Ten-Year Crush Series
My Ten-Year Crush
My Lucky Night
My Paris Romance
My Spanish Romance
My French Wedding Date
My Perfect Happy Ending

Other Books
The Match Faker

Losing My Inhibitions
Love Offline

Box Set
Ready To Mingle Collection

The Middle-Aged Virgin

Have you read my debut novel ***The Middle-Aged Virgin***? It features Sophia and Lorenzo from *My Perfect Happy Ending*! Here's what it's about:

Newly Single And Seeking Spine-Tingles…

Sophia seems to have it all: a high-flying job running London's coolest beauty PR agency, a long-term boyfriend and a dressing room filled with designer shoes. But money can't buy everything…

When tragedy strikes, Sophia realises she's actually an unhappy workaholic in a relationship that's about as exciting as a bikini wax. And as for her sex life, it's been so long since Sophia's had any action, her bestie has started calling her a *Middle-Aged Virgin*.

Determined to get a life and *get lucky*, Sophia hatches a plan to work less and live more. She ends her relationship and jets off on a cooking holiday in Tuscany, where she meets mysterious chef Lorenzo. Tall, dark and very handsome, this Italian stallion might be just what Sophia needs to spice things up in the bedroom…

But the dating scene has changed since Sophia was last single, and although she'd score an A+ for her career, when it comes to men, she's completely out of her comfort zone. How will Sophia, a self-confessed control freak, handle the unpredictable world of dating? And how much will she sacrifice for love?

Join Sophia today on her laugh-out-loud adventures as she

searches for happiness, enjoys passion between the sheets and experiences OMG moments along the way!

Here's what readers are saying about it:

"I couldn't put the book down. It's **one of the best romantic comedies I've read**." Amazon reader

"Life-affirming and empowering." Chicklit Club

"Perfect holiday read." Saira Khan, TV presenter & newspaper columnist

"Olivia has an innate knack for the sex scenes, which are very hot. **This book was steamy**, but with such a huge element of humour in it that when you read it **you will certainly giggle throughout at the escapades**." Book Mad Jo

"Absolutely hilarious! A diverse, wise and poignant novel." The Writing Garnet

Buy *The Middle-Aged Virgin* from Amazon today!

AN EXTRACT FROM THE MIDDLE-AGED VIRGIN

Prologue

'It's over.'

I did it.

I said it.

Fuck.

I'd rehearsed those two words approximately ten million times in my head—whilst I was in the shower, in front of the mirror, on my way to and from work…probably even in my sleep. But saying them out loud was far more difficult than I'd imagined.

'What the fuck, Sophia?' snapped Rich, nostrils flaring. 'What do you mean, it's over?'

As I stared into his hazel eyes, I started to ask myself the same question.

How could I be ending the fifteen-year relationship with the guy I'd always considered to be the one?

I felt the beads of sweat forming on my powdered forehead and warm, salty tears trickling down my rouged cheeks, which now felt like they were on fire. This was serious. This was actually happening.

Shit. I said I'd be strong.

'Earth to Sophia!' screamed Rich, stomping his feet.

I snapped out of my thoughts. Now would probably be a good time to start explaining myself. Not least because the veins currently throbbing on Rich's forehead appeared to indicate that he was on the verge of spontaneous combustion. Easier said than done, though, as with every second that passed, I realised the enormity of what I was doing.

The man standing in front of me wasn't just a guy that came in pretty packaging. Rich was kind, intelligent, successful, financially secure, and faithful. He was a great listener and had been there for me through thick and thin. Qualities that, after numerous failed Tinder dates, my single friends had repeatedly vented, appeared to be rare in men these days.

Most women would have given their right and probably their left arm too for a man like him. So why the hell was I suddenly about to throw it all away?

Want to find out what happens next? Buy *The Middle-Aged Virgin* from Amazon today!

ACKNOWLEDGEMENTS

I'm so incredibly grateful to the people who were involved behind the scenes and helped me bring this book to life. A massive, heartfelt thank-you goes to:

- **My amazing husband**: When I was on the fence, debating whether to write this book, your enthusiasm for my ideas was infectious. Thanks for encouraging me to go for it!
- **My fantastic beta readers: Mum, Jas, Emma, Loz** and **Brad.** *Merci* for your brilliant feedback and the love you showed for Cassie, Nico and all of the *My Ten-Year Crush* characters throughout the whole series!
- **Rachel:** for the gorgeous illustration and cover design.
- **Eliza:** for your eagle-eyed, excellent editing skills.
- **Helen:** for your great proofreading.
- **Dawn:** for keeping my website looking pretty.

- **Jay:** for giving me an insight into the emotions you went through when your beautiful child was born.
- **Jo:** for your medical expertise and sharing your experiences of pregnancy and giving birth to your adorable little one.
- **The brilliant bloggers, Bookstagrammers, ARC readers** and **BookTokers** who read and wrote lovely reviews for this book.
- And **to YOU, dear reader**. Thank you from the bottom of my heart for continuing to buy and read my books. Your continued support means the world!

Lots of love,
Olivia x

ABOUT THE AUTHOR

Olivia Spring was born and raised in London, England. When she's not making regular trips to Spain and Italy to indulge in paella, pasta, pizza and gelato, she can be found at her desk, writing new sexy romantic comedies.

If you'd like to say hi, email olivia@oliviaspring.com or connect on social media.

TikTok: www.tiktok.com/@oliviaspringauthor

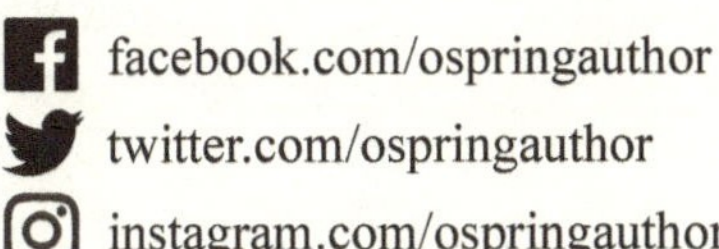

facebook.com/ospringauthor

twitter.com/ospringauthor

instagram.com/ospringauthor